Deadly Pranks

Donald Rush

Deadly Pranks

Table of Contents

~~~~~~

Chapter 1

~~~~~~~

Kirtland, Ohio

Children always think they are invincible. Jake and his friends, Kenny, Tony, and Pete thought they were.

One day Jake was standing up riding his bicycle, peddling as fast as he could, when suddenly his foot slipped off the peddle, sending him careening down onto the crossbar of his bike, and causing him to crash into a ditch. After a brief pause to let the pain lessen, Jake stood up and got right back on his bicycle, and peddled away like nothing ever happened.

That's the way it is with children. Jake could have been injured in that accident, but he did not have the common sense to understand what had even happened. Jake and his friends never thought anything bad could ever happen to them, but as they would later discover, they were dead wrong.

Kirtland is a tiny city in Northeast Ohio. Back in the sixties, there were two elementary schools, one middle school and the Kirtland High School, home of the Fighting Hornets. The typical graduating high school class size was around 100 students, making it easy to meet and become friends with nearly everyone.

For most children, growing up in Kirtland was a pleasant experience. Why did everything seem so perfect? Like every other suburb back in the sixties, the fathers were the breadwinners and went to work every day, without fail. Everyone seemed to live the same as their neighbors, in a modest ranch style home on one acre in a secluded area. Though not extravagant, it seemed to be a picture-perfect lifestyle.

Famous for being the early headquarters of the Latter-Day Saints, the township of Kirtland sits approximately 20 miles southeast of Cleveland, where Joseph Smith, along with members of his congregation, built the first Mormon Temple.

Chillicothe Road, otherwise known as State Route 306, runs directly through the center of Kirtland and alongside the high school and the original elementary school. The tree-lined street was idyllic throughout the year, until winter's frigid spell was cast upon the town. Kirtland sits directly in the middle of the snow belt and normally is pounded with snow each winter. The summers are often hot and humid. However, the spring and fall seasons are spectacularly beautiful.

Jake was about twelve years old when he began delivering the Cleveland newspaper to about thirty homes on Locust Drive. Most everyone treated Jake well, including the rare times he delivered his newspapers a little late or perhaps a little soggy from the snow or rain. Sometimes Pete assisted Jake on his paper route, especially those times when the boys had plans with Kenny and Tony and were running longer than expected. The four boys were inseparable.

Tony was the same age as Jake. On a dare, Tony would do just about anything. He seemed to have no fear. For example, Jake was afraid of heights. Tony would jump off the roof of a house or climb the tallest tree in the neighborhood with the slightest provocation.

Tony was very fast and hard to catch. He was very tough for his age.

Jake was chubby and not nearly as fast as the other boys. However, he was incredibly strong for his age. He could lift as much weight as boys two or three years older than him. Because of Jake's size, most kids did not mess with him. Jake enjoyed playing sports with the others. Although strong, he was not well coordinated. When playing football, Jake would either hike the ball or carry it up the middle. Jake took pride in being difficult to tackle.

Kenny was the oldest boy. He was tall, thin, and loved living life on the edge. He had a devious mind and did things the others would not. Later in life, this would come back to haunt him.

Pete was the youngest boy in the group and always had a sympathetic ear for everyone. Pete loved the outdoors and could rarely be found at home. Pete was most often in the woods surrounding the neighborhood. Pete was a good fighter. He was very scrappy and loved hitting hard and fast. Occasionally Pete and Jake would play their guitars in Pete's bedroom. They sounded horrible, but still managed to have fun.

During the summer, the boys normally spent the entire day outside, playing baseball, football or kick the can. Now and then, the kids on their street played football against kids from other streets in Kirtland.

The boys could sleep outside pretty much anytime they wanted to. Either their parents were very trusting, or they enjoyed the peace and quiet. The boys would usually hike up into the Gildersleeve Mountains, set up camp around Table Rock, start a fire and cook their dinner, usually consisting of hotdogs and roasted marshmallows. Sometimes the boys would swipe a watermelon from the local farmer's lot or country store.

In the wintertime, the boys might have a snowball fight or build an igloo to stay warm. Occasionally, they would have a BB gun fight. I can tell you from personal experience, those BB's hurt like hell when they hit you, especially when it was cold outside. Among all the boys, Jake was the best shot. He was remarkably accurate with his BB Gun and could easily pick off either a bird or a chipmunk.

Monday was spaghetti dinner night at Tony's house and everyone was invited. His mom Florence made a great sauce with meatballs the size of tennis balls. She often made enough spaghetti to feed ten kids. Cooking was her passion. Any of the neighborhood kids could stop by almost any time for a piece of apple strudel or peach cobbler.

It is difficult to determine exactly when things began to go negative for the boys. In their early teens, the small pranks became more cunning and bold. The group also became more vindictive.

One day, Jake was delivering papers past a home that was right on the corner of Locust Drive and Chillicothe Road when suddenly, a German shepherd attacked and nearly bit him. Jake was so frightened that he ran across the highway without looking in either direction. He might have been killed.

The owner of the German shepherd had a Cadillac. And so, Jake and Tony decided to get some payback. They called a service station a few miles away and told them to tow away the Cadillac. As the tow truck lifted the car and began to pull away, the resident, an older man, came sprinting out of the house attempting to alert the tow truck driver, but he was too late. The Cadillac was towed to a neighboring town, and the man was forced to have a friend drive him to the service station. After paying for the tow, the man was finally able to take his Cadillac home. Jake and Tony thought that was hilarious, however, the man never found out whom or why the tow truck was called, so nobody ever learned a lesson. The boys enjoyed bragging to their other friends about pranking this man, never realizing he was living on a fixed income and could not afford to buy all his medications and pay for the tow.

Chapter 2

~~~~~~~~

Silly Pranks

One Saturday afternoon, Jake, now fourteen years old, was in the middle of his paper route when Pete pulled alongside him and stopped.

Jake said, "Hey buddy, what's up?"

Pete replied, "I thought we were going to the mall today."

Jake replied, "I'm only half-finished delivering papers."

"When are you going to stop delivering these stupid papers?" said Pete.

Jake shrugged his shoulders and replied, "It's the only way I can make a few bucks. I hate asking my old man for money."

Pete laughed and asked for half the remaining papers. "I'll meet you back at your house as soon as I'm finished," said Pete. Jake smiled, nodded his head, and rode off.

Twenty minutes later, Pete and Jake met up per the agreed plan. Pete said, "Where's Kenny and Tony? I thought they were coming along."

By now the boys were accustomed to using vulgar language with each other.

"Screw em," said Jake. I'm not waiting for those douchebags to finish diddling each other."

Pete started laughing aloud. The boys all had nicknames for each other, none of which were very nice.

Just as Pete and Jake began riding towards Chillicothe Road, they spotted their friends.

As Kenny and Tony approached, Jake said, "Which one of you ladies was on top this time?"

Kenny smiled and replied, "Hey Buttercup, don't make me get off my bike and kick the shit out of you." Everyone laughed and began the five-mile bike ride to the Great Lakes Mall.

Once arriving at the mall, and for no reason, the boys went into a department store and began looking for things to steal. None of them were accomplished thieves, but all of them managed to swipe a pocket knife and a couple of cigarette lighters each.

Upon leaving the store Kenny said, "Let's go to the parking lot and see if we can steal some stuff from some of the unlocked cars."

"What kind of stuff?" asked Pete.

Kenny replied, "Just stuff like cigarettes and maybe loose change, that kind of stuff."

As usual, none of the boys could turn down a chance for a thrill.

The boys began searching for unlocked cars. Back in those days, it was not unusual for people to keep their cars unlocked. The boys found a treasure trove of items including a couple of packs of cigarettes and a handful of loose change. The boys did not seem to have a care in the world.

Having completed their mission, the boys started walking towards their bicycles, each puffing on a cigarette, when suddenly, a police car rapidly approached. A detective flung open his door and gathered the boys into a tight group. All the boys were scared shitless.

In a very deep and alarming voice, Detective Carney said, "We've been watching you boys for about an hour. What do you think you're doing?" Then, Detective Carney turned to ask a uniformed officer if he had frisked the boys yet. All four boys were literally shaking in their shoes. They all had pocket knives and other stolen items on them. The Detective continued, "Alright, since nobody is going to tell us what you were doing, we're going to drive all of you to the police station and call your parents."

With that, Kenny began speaking, "We're sorry sir. We didn't mean anyone any harm. We were just looking inside the cars for a couple of cigarettes. We know it was wrong and we promise not to do it again." All four boys began vigorously nodding their heads in unison.

Hearing that, Detective Carney turned to one of the uniformed police officers and said, "Get their names and phone numbers. Maybe I will call their parents tonight or then again, maybe I won't. But, one thing is for sure, if we ever catch any of you boys taking things from parked cars again, you will be going to jail. Understand?"

The boys told the detective they understood then quickly walked over to their bikes and speedily rode back to Kirtland. As far as the boys knew, the police never called their parents and it was never mentioned between them again.

You might think that the youngsters would have learned their lesson, but they did not. This was the turning point when the boys felt they could get away with just about anything, and their negative behavior only began to escalate.

Tony came up with the idea for the most disgusting prank ever. The boys picked up dog crap and filled the inside of one of Kenny's mom's old purses. Then they rode their bikes to the mall. After dropping the purse next to one of the parking spots, they hid and waited for someone to take the bait. It did not take very long. A young couple came along, spotted the purse, picked it up and drove off. As expected, the passenger opened the car window and flung the purse out. The boys were in tears from laughing so hard.

That was not the end of using dog crap as a prank. Sometimes the boys would put some dog crap inside the change return slot of a phone booth or under the mouthpiece of the phone. It seemed just about everyone inserted their finger into the coin return slot, looking for loose change. Tony and the others would patiently wait for someone to come along so they could get their laughs for the day. The boys also got their kicks from waiting for someone to use the phone, smell the foul odor coming from the mouthpiece, then get away as fast as possible. The boys thought they were pranking people like on the TV show "Candid Camera". However, they were doing some very nasty pranks, and they were not funny at all. Soon the boys would cross the line and cause real damage.

Chapter 3

Devious Minds

During the 1960's, there were several homes under construction on Locust Drive. Pete came up with the idea of wiring the master bedroom of the newly constructed home for sound. Pete planted a tiny microphone in the master bedroom and ran wires all the way out to the woods. Then he attached the wires to a speaker and waited for their new neighbors to move into the home. They did not have to wait very long before a young couple moved into the house. The lady of the house was a definite hottie and the boys enjoyed the sounds coming from that bedroom.

Pete told the group one night, "Too bad we can't see inside the bedroom. That might be fun to watch."

Smiling, Tony spoke up, "I can show you some pictures of your mom if you'd like."

"Shut the hell up you little bitch, or I will mess you up," replied Pete.

Everyone rolled around laughing. It was understood that any of the boys could say anything he felt like saying, and nobody would get pissed off.

Eventually the fun wore off and Pete cut the wires and destroyed the evidence. This was just one more thing the four boys got away with.

Kenny had the bright idea to pick up the swing set from the elementary school and carry it all the way out to State Route 306, then place it in the middle of the road.

Once the swing set was on the road, Jake said, "You know, this is plain wrong and stupid. If someone gets hurt or killed, it's all our asses."

"Quit being a pussy," said Kenny.

Visibly agitated, Jake responded, "I'm not a pussy. I'm just not as mentally ill as you are."

Tony said, "Jake is right. This is over the top, even for you Kenny." Tony continued, "Jake, grab a side and let's move these swings off the road."

Kenny said, "Fine, let's move them off the road. Hey, how about it if we sit them on the football field?"

Jake replied with a shrug, "That sounds like fun to me."

Then, all four boys picked up the swing set and placed it directly on the 50-yard line.

"I like this much better," said Jake.

A few days later, the boys decided it might be fun to throw apples, stolen from the farmer's lot, at passing cars. The four youngsters took a bag of apples and hid in the woods where nobody could see them. After throwing several apples and missing their targets each time, the kids came up with an alternate plan. The boys cut branches off a tree and sharpened one end. Then each boy stuck an apple onto a sharpened stick and while holding the opposite end of the stick, began flinging the apples towards cars on the highway. The boys had no comprehension that they might cause an accident and possibly hurt someone.

Kenny said, "Watch this. I think I have the timing down."

Kenny stuck an apple onto the branch and flung it, as hard as he could. "SMASH!" The sound of broken glass echoed around them.

Hearing the noise, the kids tore ass towards the graveyard and hid behind some tombstones to get a better look.

"Oh my God, I hope nobody got hurt," said Pete.

All four boys crept closer to the road to get a better look. From their vantage point, the kids could see a car sitting off to the side of the road with a broken rear window.

"Told you I had this one," said Kenny with a cocky grin.

Everyone giggled, except for Jake. He was the only boy with common sense enough to understand the implications of breaking the window of a car driving down the highway.

One time, at a school function, a young boy was on stage singing a song, "I Wish I Were a Rich Man" from "Fiddler on the Roof". Nonchalantly, Jake flipped a penny on stage. The penny rolled around the stage coming to rest at the singer's feet, causing him to cry and run off the stage. A teacher witnessed the prank and soon Jake and his pals were summoned to the principal's office to receive their punishment. Under intense grilling, and rather than ratting out Jake, all the boys willingly took the corporal punishment. A couple of whacks never bothered any of them.

Just for fun, Jake and Tony planted vegetable seeds in the football field, directly in the middle of the field. Tony also placed an old toilet alongside the freshly planted lettuce, corn, carrots, and green beans. It was thought the maintenance crew removed the vegetables from the field once they began sprouting, but that rumor was never confirmed, and nobody took credit for the stunt.

The following winter, the boys decided to throw snowballs at moving vehicles on the highway. Kenny, who brought along a couple of ice balls, said to the others, "Watch this!" then threw an ice ball so hard it hit the window of the cab of a fast-moving tractor trailer, shattered into pieces and hit the driver in the face. The driver slammed on the brakes, nearly jackknifing his rig. Coming to a stop, the driver jumped out of the cab and began to chase the boys. Fortunately for them, they had enough of a head start to get away.

Afterward, Jake said to Kenny, "Jesus Kenny! You could have killed that guy. We all need to be more careful before someone gets hurt and we end up in jail or the Juvenile Detention Center."

Kenny immediately responded to Jake, "Stop being a dick head!"

The pranks played by the kids only became more brave and stupid after that.

One of the worst things ever contributed to the four boys, although they deny it to this day, was breaking windows at the high school. One night, rocks broke nearly every window. Some of the rocks were thrown so hard the chalkboards in the front of the classrooms also shattered. The following morning, the principal was on the loudspeaker asking for help catching the criminals, though nobody at Kirtland High would ever rat someone out, least of all any of the suspected perpetrators. The principal promised that those guilty required psychiatric help and he would make sure they received it. He possibly was correct, but the culprits were never discovered.

The following spring, Kenny, Jake, Tony and Pete all turned sixteen, fifteen, fifteen, and fourteen years old, respectively, and certainly old enough to understand right from wrong.

Occasionally, Florence would send the boys to the fruit stand to pick up apples for a pie. Of course, Tony put the money in his pocket and the boys went to the orchard to just steal the fruit. During the fall, the boys went on several successful fruit raids. By now, the farmer had become aware of these little delinquents and was attempting to catch them. Several times, after witnessing the thieves take fruit, the farmer drove his car towards them, only to watch them run away.

During April, things really got out of hand. The boys were planning to camp out so they needed some food. Kenny said to the others, "It's getting dark out, time to raid the farmer's lot!"

All four boys agreed, and off they went. Upon arriving at the orchard, each boy began filling their sacks up with grapes, apples, pears, peaches, and plums.

If not for the headlights, the boys may have been caught. Jake spotted the car speeding towards them and he alerted everyone to the advancing danger. The boys dropped their stolen booty and ran. The farmer, unable to drive any further because the apple trees blocked his path, stopped and flew out of his car then gave chase on foot. The farmer was an older man, but in very good shape and much faster than the boys thought he would be. As usual, Kenny, Pete and Tony were far ahead while Jake lagged behind. He was certain he was going to be caught. Kenny and Pete stopped running and lifted the top row of the barbed wire so that Jake could slip through. Once all four boys were safely back on Locust Drive, they hid in the woods to catch their breath, and waited for the danger to subside.

Tony was having some difficulty breathing and took a couple pulls from his inhaler. The tightness in his chest subsided almost immediately. The boys spotted the farmer's car driving down the street, attempting to locate even one of the culprits. The farmer continued to drive around the block several more times before giving up and heading home.

Instead of being happy they avoided capture, the boys were pissed off and vowed revenge. A few days later, armed with knives and razor blades, all four boys returned to the farmer's lot and cut smiley faces in as many apples they could reach then began kicking the hell out of dozens of watermelons. Jake stood lookout from close to the fence and kept watch for the farmer, while the others did their dirty deeds. Although Jake did not voice his opinion, he thought this retaliation was both disturbing and unnecessary.

Things changed after that. Kenny, Pete and Tony's behavior rapidly became more angry and more vengeful. Jake, however, became considerably more cautious because he feared their crimes could one day come back to haunt them.

While camping out about a week later, the boys decided to break into a gas station. After breaking a small window on the gas station door, the boys managed to unlock the door and enter. Once inside, the boys broke into the cigarette, snack, and soft drink machines taking more than twenty packs of cigarettes and a load of snacks. Altogether, they stole over $30.00 in change from the vending machines.

Now, safely back at their campground, Kenny laid out the plans for future break-ins, including a resort and a second gas station.

The following weekend, Kenny told everyone it was time to break into the resort. This resort was closed for the season. However, there was still plenty of food in the freezer. Jake and Tony entered the freezer and stole four porterhouse steaks. Meanwhile, Kenny and Pete broke open the vending machines and swiped more cigarettes and change. Jake was a little anxious about this robbery because he knew the owner of the resort personally. Tony kept the steaks in his parent's freezer and the following weekend, the boys cooked their steaks over the open campfire. Everyone seemed to enjoy their dinner reliving the adventure by which they acquired their steaks.

By now, the boys could see extra patrol cars around the area. Because the dollar amount of each crime was small, the police were certain juvenile offenders committed these robberies. After all, loose change and cigarettes are something a kid or a teenager might steal. The police were now on the lookout for small gangs of older boys or teenagers.

Jake did his best to convince the other boys to lay low for a couple of weeks. He told them about the increase in patrols around Kirtland, including Locust Drive. He could not help but think the police were following him and his friends. Maybe Jake was paranoid, but then again, why take the chance? None of the boys wanted to let their parents down. In a small town like Kirtland, being a suspect in a robbery would hurt all their parents.

With summer rapidly approaching an end, Kenny considered breaking into homes of people in the area who were on vacation. At first, Jake wanted no part of this and tried to stay out of it as much as possible.

Kenny said to Jake, "Hey buddy, you deliver newspapers so you know who is on vacation and who is home. Just give us this information and you won't have to do the robberies and we'll still cut you in."

Jake nodded his head and replied, "Sure, I'll give you the information but if you get caught, keep me out of it."

"Look, I'm not trying to hurt your feelings," said Kenny. "If someone tries to catch us, we can run faster than you. It would be better if you kept watch."

"That's fine," said Jake. "The Olson family is away for two weeks. I don't know what they have worth stealing but go for it."

Tony, Pete, and Kenny were planning to break into the Olsen home the upcoming Saturday evening. The Friday night before, the four boys gathered at their campground to discuss the plan, however, what happened next would never allow the gang to pull this one off.

Chapter 4

Roberts Family

Euclid Chardon Road, also known as State Route 6, runs west between Kirtland, through Chardon, Ohio, and all the way into Pennsylvania. The Roberts' farm, built by William Roberts shortly after the end of World War I, sat on about forty acres of excellent farm land, about one mile west of highway 306, and as an extra bonus, contained a large freshwater pond, located in the center of the property.

William never enjoyed living in the city and he always felt the pace was a little too fast for him. He wanted to be able to stretch his legs, as he would say, and desperately wanted to own a piece of land he could farm. He vowed to one day do just that. He only needed to save up the money, a challenge back in those days.

William was too young to enter the military when the First World War began in 1917. However, he landed a job as a machinist. William never liked running a machine, but he was good at it and made some decent money. William saved most of his money so one day he might realize his dream.

William met Sarah Meadows in 1920 and the two quickly fell in love and soon married. William was elated his wife envisioned a similar future that he did. Even though the couple knew farming would be hard work, they continued saving their money until they could eventually buy the farm in Kirtland, Ohio.

In 1922, William and Sarah were blessed with a child, a son they named Jack, after Sarah's father. By the time Jack was old enough to enter school, he was working the farm. Jack would often rise early, play around on the farm until time to go to school, come home, do his homework then help wherever his father needed him. Jack loved feeding the animals, milking the cows, gathering the eggs, as well as picking apples for his mother to bake a pie.

Jack grew up on the farm. He had a wonderful work ethic and by the time he finished high school, he was planting and growing his own crops such as lettuce, beans, blackberries, and peaches. Jack built a small fruit stand near the intersection of Chillicothe and Euclid Chardon Road, where he occasionally transported his produce to sell.

Shortly after the Japanese attacked Pearl Harbor in December 1941, Jack, along with tens of thousands of other young men, enlisted in the Army. Jack was keen on learning to drive heavy equipment and as he gained skill, he was recruited to assist building bridges and airstrips. Jack was a large-scale thinker. He thought, providing he survived the war, heavy equipment experience might help him later in life. At that time, he was nineteen years old, fearless and in the best shape of his life.

In June 1945, Jack was sent to Okinawa to assist building an airstrip. The Battle of Okinawa was nearly over and the United States urgently needed this airstrip. From Okinawa, America could launch attacks by air against places as far away as Tokyo. The Battle of

Okinawa lasted about eighty-one days, resulting in thousands of casualties.

Like every other soldier, Jack wanted to go home, but more importantly, wanted to see the end of the war. Jack hated hearing the high number of allied casualties, and for this reason, felt honored to be in Okinawa, building the new airstrip.

When the airstrip was almost completed, a lone Japanese sniper, taking several shots at the construction workers, shot Jack in the leg. The bullet hit a bone, shattering upon impact. The Army doctors, unable to remove the entire bullet, left fragments inside his leg. Although in constant pain, Jack continued to assist building the airstrip. Eventually, Jack's leg became infected and he was discharged from the Army and sent home. The doctors in Cleveland also tried but failed to remove the bullet fragments. Jack always said getting shot in the leg hurt like hell. Years later, if someone looked closely, they could see the traces of the remaining bullet fragments.

Jack met Katherine, his future wife, during leave in Hawaii in 1942. Raised in rural Cambridge, Minnesota, Katherine was not only pretty but she was also a very hard worker. Katherine could not wait to start their new lives. The idea of working a farm intrigued her and soon after Jack's medical discharge, they headed for the family farm in Kirtland.

Jack and Katherine helped William on the farm, learning every possible aspect of farming. After a few years of hard work, William and Jack purchased their first tractor. Now, Jack's experience driving heavy equipment came in very handy.

Jack and Katherine spent most of their time together and could usually be found working the land or tending for the animals. They felt blessed for their wonderful life.

In 1946, Katherine gave birth to Kimberly, their first of two daughters. Only three years later, Sally was born.

William, Jack and their families prospered and they eventually purchased a second forty-acre parcel of land that was adjacent to theirs.

After Sally's birth, William and Jack built a second house on the adjacent parcel of land. The new house was smaller than the main house and William and

Sarah decided to move into it. Now, Jack, Katherine and their two children resided in the larger home.

Between both families, they were now working nearly eighty acres. The main farm was dedicated to growing corn and apples while the new parcel housed various fruits including watermelons, blackberries and strawberries. By now, Jack was running most of the day-to-day operations while William took care of the business side including accounts payable and receivable. Eventually, Jack built several small dwellings or cabins on the second parcel of land, a place for their hired seasonal helpers to reside.

Things went well for several years until William began laboring to breathe. Stubborn to a fault, William eventually agreed to visit the hospital for a checkup and discovered he was suffering from advanced lung disease, attributed to years of breathing in dust and pesticides on the farm. From then on, Jack ran the entire operation and Katherine took over the books. Katherine was a natural at bookkeeping and loved the work. William assisted where he could or when he felt well enough to do so. Still, the farm ran very well. Jack brought in new ideas and techniques using his construction skill and experience. Jack built an excellent sprinkler system to help irrigate their crops, where he utilized the water from their own natural water supply. Now, after turning on a series of powerful pumps, the water flowed to their crops effortlessly. The local farmers were envious and William was very impressed and proud of Jack. He knew the farm was being left into very capable hands.

By now, the farm owned or leased several tractors used to help plow the fields or harvest the corn. Automation was a lifesaver. Jack became more of a manager, directing his farm hands on their day-to-day duties.

William, now a shell of the man he once was, passed away at the young age of 55. Jack was very close to his father and grieved for many months. Sarah remained in the second home where she passed her time baking, taking care of the grandchildren and quilting. Sarah passed away three years later; some say from a broken heart.

In 1960, although never smoking a day in her life, Jack's wife Katherine was diagnosed with lung cancer and died only six months later. Jack was heartbroken. So were the girls. By now, the children were a bit older and Jack could spend most of his time attending the farm. Jack decided it was time to hire an accountant to care for the business duties of running the farm.

In 1963, Kimberly turned seventeen years old and Sally was fourteen. Both girls were very smart and proficient working the farm. Kimberly, a recent high school graduate, was very tall at 5' 10" and Sally was a little shorter and a bit heavier, making her self-conscious about her weight. Folks always told Sally not to worry about her weight. However, she could not wait until she was as tall as her sister was. Both girls were very pretty and unusually ambitious. Day in and day out, seven nights a week, they prepared dinner for their father while also keeping up the housework and their homework. The girls were not afraid to get their hands dirty and often assisted with farm duties whenever possible.

Jack took pride in his work and was a good provider for his two daughters. Jack adored his girls and did his best to make sure they had everything they wanted, within reason. When Kimberly turned sixteen, she asked her father for her driver's license. Not only did Kimberly get her license, she also received a very sweet used Chevy Van. Kimberly could not believe her good fortune and vowed never to be careless with her vehicle. Sally was happy for her sister because she knew they would be going places together such as the movies or the mall. Sally also hoped in another year or two, she might get her own vehicle, especially since she was an honor roll student.

Jack often spoke to his daughters about attending college and he hoped the girls might one day attend the Ohio State University, his favorite college. Jack never attended college himself, but he adored the Buckeyes football team along with famed coach Woody Hayes. Neither girl was overly excited at the thought of college. However, they both desired to please their father. Kimberly was old enough to attend college and her grades were certainly good enough, however, she lacked the desire to leave home. Jack finally caved in and told the girls they could attend the local community college where they could take some of their required classes then maybe settle on a college later. This pleased both girls very much. They always seemed to get their way but they both wanted to stay close to home because their father was working so hard and they were concerned about him.

During the apple-picking season, Jack frequently hired a couple of additional workers. The job was just too much work and his other employees were already busy. Jack knew his children were doing their best and they already had full plates.

One evening, Jack arrived home, breathing a little harder than normal, to tell his daughters about four boys he again chased off the farm. Over the past month or so, Jack ran these kids off his property several times. However, they kept returning. Jack hoped the boys finally got the lesson.

The morning of apple picking season began as usual. As the apples on the lower branches of one tree came into view, Jack's normally pleasant demeanor turned to anger as he spotted several cut up and destroyed apples. Jack turned his attention to the watermelon patch. Dozens and dozens of his watermelons were also destroyed. Jack was enraged with anger, and suddenly felt a tightness in his chest that he had never experienced before. One of the farm hands drove Jack to the house, asking the girls to keep an eye on him. Shortly after arriving home, Jack began gasping for air. He quickly told his daughters about what the boys did to their apples and watermelons. Sensing he was in serious trouble, Jack quickly said, "I love you both very much," then passed away quietly in front of his children.

Kimberly and Sally were still overwhelmed with grief from their mother's death several years earlier, and both girls often cried aloud. Kimberly worried the death of their father might be too much to bear.

The farm's accountant came over to speak with the girls shortly after the funeral. As it turned out, Jack had provided for his children very well. The farm was paid off, free and clear. There were no other loans or mortgages of any concern, plus, Jack left his daughters as co-beneficiaries of his estate along with his ample life insurance policy.

Somehow, owning the farm plus having a few dollars did not seem to matter very much. Although they were grateful for their newfound wealth, there was an emptiness inside both girls they constantly spoke about when they were alone together in the evenings.

One morning before Sally left for school, Kimberly approached her and said, "Do you think you know who these boys might be, the ones who destroyed the fruit and our lives?"

Sally replied, "I'd love to know their names, and if I ever find out who they are, I just might kill them myself. But no, I don't know who they are."

Kimberly then approached Sally and very calmly said, "While you are at school, day after day, pay close attention to anyone who might be bragging about destroying our fruit and watch out for a small pack of boys who always seem to be together." Kimberly continued, "Every night after school, we will drive around all the streets in the immediate area and look for possible suspects. We will drive up and down Billings Road, Eagle, Gildersleeve, Sperry, Wisner Road and Locust Drive. Someone, somewhere will know something and we'll be able to locate the group responsible, and God help them if we do."

Puzzled, Sally looked at Kimberly and asked, "What are you planning to do if we ever find them?"

Kimberly smiled with an evil grin and said, "You'll have to wait and see. First, let's find these bastards."

Chapter 5

Finding Pete

After taking a brief sabbatical from school, Sally returned to Kirtland High School to continue her studies. Sally felt she owed it to her father to graduate high school then possibly attend college. Sally had many friends at school. She was always popular, especially with her infectious smile and demeanor. These days, however, Sally kept mostly to herself because she had difficulty talking about her father's death. Most of Sally's friends understood her grief and kept their distance.

One morning, just before her history class with Mr. Thrasher, Sally overheard a conversation that would change her forever. Pete Peterson, a boy in her class, was telling several other boys about raiding a farmer's lot, getting chased then going back to retaliate. Pete did not know Sally. In fact, they ran in different circles. Sally could not help but glare at Pete. First, she became angry then sick to her stomach and eventually rose from her chair and walked out of class. All heads turned as Sally left the classroom, but then again most of the kids understood she was struggling emotionally. Sally went to the nurse's office and explained she was experiencing stomach pain and asked for an excuse to go home. Right away, Sally called Kimberly and asked her to come to the school to pick her up. Immediately, Kimberly asked Sally what the problem was, however, Sally preferred to talk with her sister face to face. Fifteen minutes later, Kimberly arrived.

Sally was visibly shaking and crying. Kimberly was extremely concerned about her younger sister and asked her what was going on.

Sally, partly crying and partly smiling, looked at her sister and blurted out, "I think I found one of them."

Swiftly, Kimberly pulled the van over and coming to a stop, placed the vehicle in park then turned to Sally to ask, "What do you mean, you think you found one? One what? I think I know what you're talking about, but you'd better tell me right now!"

Shaking, Sally responded to Kimberly, "One of the little punks who destroyed our orchard, that's who."

Kimberly could only say, "Oh my God, are you shitting me? Tell me you are serious?"

Sally began telling Kimberly about her history class and the conversation she had overheard. She told Kimberly that she knew that the boy's first name was Pete, but she did not know his last name or where he lived.

Kimberly calmly responded, "Let's head home and talk about this."

Sally nodded in agreement but could not help but weep all the way home.

Later that evening, during dinner, both girls were unusually quiet. Kimberly eventually broke the ice and said to Sally, "Why are you so quiet? Don't you want to get even for the boys killing our father?"

Looking up from her plate, Sally responded, "I definitely want to do something to them, but I don't want to go to prison either."

Kimberly replied, "I understand. Let's open a bottle of wine and discuss our options. This is a special occasion."

"Seriously, you're going to let me have some wine?" asked Sally.

Kimberly smiled and began to pour the wine. Kimberly really wanted a drink and both girls needed one to calm their nerves.

After drinking the white wine, Kimberly asked Sally if she might have any ideas how to get some payback.

Sally casually told her sister, "Actually I have been thinking of a few things, although all my ideas are extremely cruel. Not that they don't deserve it though." Sally continued, "Since the boys seem to like watermelon, we could dig a vertical hole in the watermelon patch and bury them up to their necks. We would have to gag them and keep a hood over their heads. I'm sure they would love having ants and bugs crawling all over their face."

Kimberly looked at her sister. "What a dreadful little bitch you've become." With that, both girls busted up laughing.

"Pour me another glass of wine," said Sally.

"Easy there, I don't want you to become a raging wino," laughed Kimberly, calmly picking up the wine bottle and pouring each of them another glass.

"Alright," said Sally. "What's your big idea to get rid of these vermin?"

"Alright, here goes," said Kimberly. "We bring them into the barn, hang them upside down, cut their pathetic nut sack, one slice every day until their useless acorns fall off."

Sally was rolling around laughing her butt off. Smiling ear to ear, Sally said to Kimberly, "And you call me a terrible bitch. What about you?"

Kimberly replied, "There's always Lake Erie, only twenty miles away."

Sally said, "What do you mean, Lake Erie?"

"I mean exactly that. We capture these animals, hold them in the basement inside dog kennels and eventually take them to the lake to dispose of them," replied Kimberly.

Sally was not sure what to make of this idea, probably because it made some sense to her. "I think we should do exactly that," said Sally.

Almost serenely, Kimberly told her sister that these were some of the dark thoughts that kept her awake at night.

Kimberly said to Sally, "We need to plan this carefully. You return to school tomorrow and begin to find out everything you can about the boy named Pete. Watch him very closely. Eventually, he will lead you to the other three little bastards."

Sally was a bit tipsy but was able to respond to Kimberly, "I am going to do exactly that. Now that I know what one of them looks like, we can drive around in the evening till I spot him again. He shouldn't be too hard to find."

"Fine by me," replied Kimberly with a decided nod. "Let's start tomorrow. When we find out who they all are and where each one lives, then we can come up with a solid plan to rid ourselves of the vermin."

The girls smiled at each other as they placed their wine glasses in the kitchen and headed off to their rooms, and for the first time in months, they both went to bed and fell into a peaceful sleep.

Chapter 6

~~~~~~~~~

Spring Dance

The next day, as promised, Sally returned to school. During history class, Sally could not help but stare at Pete Peterson who seemed to notice the continuous glances and wondered if maybe Sally liked him. Pete thought he might ask Sally to dance at the upcoming school dance. After all, Sally had a great figure and was very pretty. Pete had yet to even talk to Sally. When it came to girls, he was a bit shy.

Day after day Sally kept an eye on Pete until the end of the week, when she struck pay dirt. On Friday, Pete came up to Sally and asked if he could speak with her. Sally had a lump in her throat but managed to nod her head up and down. Pete walked outside the building with Sally close behind him. Pete, after finally getting his nerve up, quickly said to Sally, "I wonder if you would go to the spring dance with me tomorrow night."

Sally was not sure what to say. Eventually, she came up with words and replied, "Let me check with my sister to make sure we don't have any plans. Can I call you tomorrow?"

"Why don't you give me your number and I'll call you," said Pete.

Thinking quickly, Sally responded, "It would be better if I call you. My sister worries about me since she's all I got and I don't want to upset her."

Pete replied, "That would be great." Writing down his phone number on a piece of paper, Pete said, "I hope to hear from you."

Sally smiled and assured Pete, "Oh yes, you will definitely hear from me."

Sally could not wait to walk out to the parking lot where Kimberly was waiting.

Sally opened the door and could barely contain herself as she hopped in the van. Hastily, Sally said, "You will not believe what happened today at school. You will never guess, not in a million years."

Grinning ear to ear as she pulled out of the parking lot, Kimberly said, "Well don't keep me in suspense. Tell me right now. You've piqued my curiosity."

Sally said, "Guess who asked me to the dance tomorrow night?"

"No way," replied Kimberly.

"Yes," said Sally. "He wants to be my date tomorrow night. I told him I'd have to speak with you first."

"Does he have a car?" asked Kimberly.

"I don't think so. I believe he just wants to meet me at the school," replied Sally.

"You should go," said Kimberly. "Meet him at school and try to be pleasant. Tell him I will pick both of you up after the dance and take you home. It will be dark out so nobody will be able to see the van or us. Don't get too close to him and never give him our phone number."

"I didn't give our number to him. I told him he had to give his number to me and I would call him tomorrow," said Sally.

Kimberly said, "That was quick thinking. The less they know about us, the better. This way we will find out where this little prick lives. Then we can begin searching for the others."

The following morning, Sally called Pete. Lucky for her, Pete answered the phone. "Hi, this is Sally. If you still want to go to the dance, I can meet you there at 7:00 pm," she said.

Pete was very pleased. He had wanted to begin dating but was always afraid to ask someone. Once he saw Sally glancing his way every now and then, he finally got the nerve up to ask. Pete did not have a driver's license yet, so asking a girl out was awkward. He still was unsure how to pull it off. "I suppose I can ask my dad to pick us up after the dance and take us home," said Pete.

Sally told Pete about her sister insisting that she be the one to pick them up after the dance, and that she would make sure they would get home all right.

"It's a date," Pete said.

"I'll meet you at the school," said Sally.

Afterward, Sally met with Kimberly to go over the night's plans.

Kimberly said, "Remember, we are not going to snatch him tonight. We only want to make him feel comfortable so he will show us exactly where he lives. It won't be long until we have identified all four creeps."

Sally nodded her head in agreement.

Later that evening, Kimberly dropped Sally off at the dance. She immediately saw that Pete was waiting for her.

Pete paid the way into the dance and even bought Sally a soda and popcorn. One time, while slow dancing, Pete's hand slowly crept a little too far south for Sally's comfort. She immediately corrected his behavior by pulling Pete's hand off her hip. Pete got the message, loud and clear. Overall, Pete was a gentleman. Sally felt a little sorry for Pete but he was one of the boys responsible for her father's death. Sally silently hoped Pete would not be tortured or even murdered. Sally was unsure how far Kimberly would take things. *I need to toughen up,* Sally thought to herself. After this night, she would never see Pete socially ever again.

After the dance, Kimberly picked both Sally and Pete up, as promised. On the way home, the conversation was friendly yet direct. Kimberly asked

Pete a few questions that a mother or father might ask a boy taking their daughter out for the first time. Questions like, where do you live, how long have you lived in Kirtland and do you have many friends here? Pete politely responded, "I've lived here most of my life, along with my younger brother and sister. I have a few friends but only three I would call close."

Sally inquired, "What's your friends' names, maybe I know them, or went to school with their siblings?"

Pete replied, "I don't think you would know them, but their names are Kenny, Jake and Tony. Kenny is two years older than I am. Jake and Tony are only one year older."

"I think I may know Tony. What's his last name?"

"His name is Tony Sawyer," replied Pete.

Kimberly replied, "No, I don't think I know him after all."

By now, the van was approaching Locust Drive. Pete asked Kimberly to turn left then he directed her to his home, even pointing out where Tony lived along the way. Everyone said goodnight and Kimberly began the short trip back to their farmhouse.

On the way home Kimberly said to Sally with a wry grin, "Pete seems pretty nice. It will almost be a shame to kill his dumb ass."

"Do we really need to kill all of them?" asked Sally.

Kimberly replied, "Well, if we kidnap them at gunpoint and we get caught, we will probably go to prison for twenty years. If we kidnap and torture them, we could go to prison for life. If we kidnap them, torture them, murder and dump their bodies in Lake Erie, we can deny everything and we might just get away with murder. Which do you think we should do?"

Sally said, "I see your point. Well, I vote we start driving around Locust Drive. Now we know where two of them live. They should be easy to find. I think it is too much of a coincidence that Pete has three friends and they are all very close and live near each other. You realize they just so happen to live right behind our orchard?"

Kimberly nodded to affirm. "Let's begin our search tomorrow at dusk."

By now the van was pulling in the driveway. Kimberly turned to her sister and said, "Get some sleep. Tomorrow could be a long day."

Chapter 7

Getting Organized

The following night after school, the girls began searching for their enemies. They began by driving around Locust Drive to get a feel for the area. During the drive, Kimberly observed a thickly wooded area almost directly across from Pete's house.

"Hey Sally, this might make a great observation spot. We can walk through the woods behind our farm and wait for Pete to meet up with his friends," said Kimberly.

Sally replied, "I agree. Pete mentioned that he and his friends were playing football this weekend at the cemetery. That might be a good time to see what the others look like."

The next night, Kimberly and Sally began driving around Locust Drive. Not wanting to be obvious, they drove around the block one time then drove home. For the entire week, Kimberly and Sally failed to have any sightings of Pete or any of his friends. Once the weekend rolled around, the sisters drove around the cemetery but never did find anyone playing football. Kimberly and Sally drove back to the cemetery on Sunday with the same results, no boys. The girls were beginning to feel discouraged.

The following Monday afternoon, Sally came home from school as usual. Kimberly was waiting for her at the door.

"I've been up the entire night thinking about what to do and I finally came up with a plan," said Kimberly.

Sally replied, "Well don't keep me in suspense. What's the new plan?"

"The boys are not going anywhere. We should spend some time on how we plan to capture these idiots and then what we plan to do with them once we accomplish that," said Kimberly.

Sally replied, "Okay, so where do we start?"

Kimberly said, "Well, spring is nearly over and that means summer will soon be here. In just a few short weeks, you will be finished with school until next year. Once school ends, these boys will probably spend time together, just like Pete told us."

"So, you think the boys will be easier to find and capture once school's out?" asked Sally.

"Absolutely. If you remember, the night of the spring dance, Pete told us he and his friends spent almost the entire summer together. Pete told us sometimes they go on vacation with each other's families or they play football, baseball or camp out. I think if we can find out where they camp out, maybe we can snatch them when they fall asleep," said Kimberly.

"That's a brilliant idea!" exclaimed Sally.

"Thank you, thank you. I do have my moments," replied Kimberly. Both girls laughed and sat down for dinner.

After dinner, Kimberly began laying out her thoughts on what to do with the Locust Drive boys. Kimberly began, "We have two farm hands living right next door. We'll tell them we are going to board up the second home for the summer to save on expenses and they will need to leave by the end of May." Kimberly continued, "We'll use the second house for our future guests. We need to drive around to find some cages, big cages. We will drive to Cincinnati, across the Ohio River into Kentucky, maybe Erie, PA. and then to Detroit, and buy one cage in each city, paying with cash."

"Why can't we buy all the cages right here in Cleveland?" asked Sally.

Kimberly responded, "If someone, like the FBI, investigates four boys missing from one street, the sale of four cages might raise a red flag. I don't know if anyone would look at that or not, but why take chances?"

"The FBI, what are you talking about? Now you're really scaring the crap out of me." Sally continued, "Jesus, you have given this a little bit of thought. At first, I thought you were not serious about doing anything but now I am not so sure. I have to tell you, it's a little scary."

"I absolutely want those little pricks to pay for what they've done," replied Kimberly. "I dream every night about how to screw with their minds, murder them and get rid of their bodies. But I need you to tell me right now, are you with me or not? Because once we get started there is no going back."

"I'm with you, always," replied Sally.

Unexpectedly, Kimberly looked directly into her sister's eyes and said; "Listen closely, I'm telling you right now. If something bad happens such as we are caught, I will take the entire blame for all of it. You just tell the police you have no idea what they're talking about." Kimberly continued, "You never went out with Pete, you never went with me to buy cages, you never did a goddamn thing. Do you understand me?"

"Yes," replied Sally. "Although that's not very fair to you."

"This is my idea, my plan and not yours. If we are captured, the first and only thing you say to the police is that you want an attorney. I am the custodian and you are a minor. I read a lot of crime books. You have rights and they cannot interrogate you without a parent or guardian present once you ask for an attorney. Do not agree to a lie detector test, ever! I will not speak to the police. I will ask for a lawyer. Promise me, you will never admit to doing anything, no matter what kind of tricks the police may try," said Kimberly.

"Alright, alright, I promise," said Sally.

"Okay, I'll talk to the farm hands tomorrow. They should vacate the second house by the end of May. We will give them some extra money so they can take a nice extended vacation."

Relieved the conversation was over, Sally left to go up to her room and do her homework, although the evening's discussion with Kimberly continued to concern her.

Chapter 8

~~~~~~~~~~

Serious Intentions

The next two weeks were hectic for Kimberly and Sally. Their plan began to take shape. By the end of May, the farmhands and their families left the premises.

Kimberly and her sister drove to the Willoughby library, sat down at a table with out of state phone books, and located several feed and grain stores in various cities. They wrote down the phone numbers and began making calls from pay phones. Kimberly did not want to make these calls from home just in case they were caught. Kimberly had a very dark and twisted mind and it almost seemed she was more than just looking forward to getting revenge. She almost seemed pleased with herself and her plans. Kimberly seemed to have an aptitude for this.

With little effort, the girls found the cages they were seeking. Almost every one of the stores they called had a suitable cage. Most of the cages were large enough to keep small boys.

The first week of June, school was out for the summer. It was time to put their plan into action. The next day Kimberly drove to one of four cities to purchase a cage. Kimberly refused to allow Sally to come along. She was concerned someone could potentially identify Sally and thought it would be better if she went alone. Sally was not pleased.

Kimberly said, "Look, I don't want you to get caught. Also, if someone sees both of us together at the same time, it could make it easier to identify one or both of us. Remember, you have nothing to do with this."

Reluctantly Sally agreed. "Fine; I'll stay at home and clean out the basement of the second home. That is where we are keeping the boys, right?"

Kimberly replied, "That's right. The cages come unassembled, so they will be easy to take down the stairs into the basement and put together. Then we can hang the black curtains between each cage. I do not want the boys to watch when we do stuff to the others. Also, do not worry about getting the basement too clean. I could care less what kind of filth they live in. I don't care if the rats and bugs eat them alive."

Sally nodded although she was beginning to worry about her older sister. She wondered to herself why Kimberly was taking this so seriously. Sally guessed that since Kimberly was older and had spent more time with their father, his death hit her harder than it did to herself. Kimberly wanted to kill every one of the boys. Her grief was wreaking havoc on her sanity.

Each morning Kimberly drove off to a new destination where she would locate the feed store, purchase the cage and bring it home. After dark, Kimberly and Sally would take the new cage downstairs and assemble it. By the end of the week, all four cages were in the basement and fully assembled.

After the cages were installed, Kimberly visited several hardware stores in the area and purchased locks, one for each cage. Kimberly kept only one key per lock. She was a little concerned Sally might lack the willpower to complete their retaliation, so she kept each key on a necklace she wore around her neck.

A few days later, Kimberly and Sally boarded up all the windows of the house, changed the master locks, and then began searching for their prey.

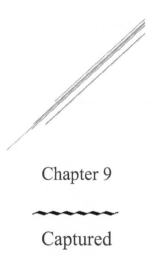

Chapter 9

Captured

Jake and his friends could hardly wait for school to end. They speculated that the following year, one or two of them would have driver's licenses. That would be sweet. Until then, it was playtime as usual on Locust Drive.

By now, the boys were finished playing nasty pranks. They only wanted to play games, lift weights, drive go-carts and camp outside.

Occasionally, Jake's mom sent the boys to the farmer's orchard to pick apples for a pie. Over time, they learned the best routes to enter the apple orchard, grab some fruit and make a quick exit. None of the boys knew they were being watched. It was business as usual for all of them.

Every Friday night, the boys hiked to Gildersleeve Mountain to camp out. Usually, they would bring pillows, sleeping bags and some dinner. After setting up the camp, they would light a small fire, cook their food, sit around the campfire roasting marshmallows and talk about things that interested them, such as girls or sports. They did not seem to have a care in the world.

It was July 5, 1963, the first Friday of the month. As usual, the boys went to the Gildersleeve Mountains to camp out. The boys brought along some M-80 fireworks, left over from the day before. Jake started the customary fire and all four boys cooked their dinner. This time they brought along leftover hotdogs and hamburgers from the July 4th picnic at the Sawyer's home. Mrs. Sawyer also made potato salad, which was always a crowd pleaser in the neighborhood. All four boys filled up their paper plates with potato salad and either a burger or a hot dog. Jake took one of each, but he was a bigger boy than the others were.

After dinner, the boys spent their time talking about cars. Everyone at the time wanted a 1957 Chevy. To each boy, this was the best car ever built. Kenny told the group he would be receiving his license later that year and hoped to have a nice car. Kenny said his father would not buy him a car until he had a part-time job to help pay the car payments and insurance. Kenny had his eye on a job at a local market. On a couple of occasions, Kenny met the owner and they seemed to get along. The owner told Kenny to come back when he turned sixteen and maybe they could find something for him to do. Kenny had dreams of a sweet car and dating one of the lovely local girls.

Pete spoke of the spring dance and Sally, the girl he took to the dance. Pete thought Sally seemed nice and she was pretty. Pete told the boys about the one slow dance when he tried to grab her ass but his hand was rejected. Everyone laughed at Pete. Pete responded, "You little homos stayed at home yanking at yourselves. At least I tried. Jake was probably busy looking at the panty section of the Sears catalog."

Jake blushed a little and replied, "You caught me. I was looking at the panty and bra section of the catalog. I heard your mom was appearing in her first photo shoot."

"Screw you, needle dick," said Pete.

"Ouch, that really hurt," replied Jake, holding his hand over his heart like he was wounded.

Everyone began laughing. When the laughing subsided, Kenny said, "Alright, I'm tired. You guys shut the hell up before I stick my fist down your throats."

Not sure if Kenny was serious, the boys all crawled into their sleeping bags and closed their eyes. None of the boys heard the noises coming from the bushes, not more than twenty yards away.

By 2:00 am, the boys were all fast asleep. Kimberly and Sally rose from their position and slowly walked towards the sleeping lads. Both Kimberly and Sally wore all black clothing including black pants, a black coat and hat, black shoes, and black gloves plus facemasks. They pulled their hair up so nobody could see who they were or even if they were men or women. Kimberly added padding to the shoulders of each coat making them seem larger than they were. In fact, they appeared more like men, not women. Both girls carried weapons, Kimberly had a sixteen-gauge shotgun and

Sally gingerly held a 38-caliber handgun, both belonging to their father. The shotgun was loaded with rock salt. The handgun was loaded with live rounds. The girls did not want to kill the boys right away, unless they were forced to. They wanted to have some fun first.

Hearing a shell being pumped into the shotgun immediately woke Jake up. Jake was familiar with the sound. His father had a shotgun and on occasion, he took all the boys out to shoot targets. Coincidentally, the targets were usually pumpkins or watermelons, stolen from the farmer's lot. Jake shook Kenny's arm then the others. The four boys were now wide-awake, staring down the barrel of a shotgun. None of the boys could speak. Their throats were dry. They were unsure of what to do. Pete and Tony both thought they were going to die. Surprisingly, Kenny did not seem so tough. He was just as frightened as the others were.

Neither Kimberly nor Sally spoke to the boys. Sally handed her pistol to Kimberly. Then, she opened a pillowcase and removed several cardboard signs from inside. Written on each sign was an order for the boys to follow. Kimberly kept the shotgun leveled at the boys. Sally held up the first sign as the boys watched in abject terror. Sally held her flashlight on the cardboard sign. It read, *If you run, you will be shot.*

Jake began, "What's going on, who the hell are …" and was abruptly cut off.

Sally quickly flipped over the next sign. It read, *Shut the fuck up. Speak again and one of you will die!*

All the boys just stood there, frozen, with their mouths open. None of them spoke or attempted to run.

Sally held up another sign. It read, *I'm going to tie each of you up. If you struggle or run, we will kill you!*

Sally went to each boy, first Kenny, followed by Jake, Tony, then Pete, and tied their hands together in front of them so they could each carry their sleeping bags and supplies. Then Sally kicked dirt on the fire to extinguish it.

Sally shined her flashlight on the next sign. It read, *Gather your pillows and sleeping bags then follow me, or we will kill you.*

Finally, the boys were tied together around their waists, single file, and led down the mountain until they reached the bottom.

Then, Sally held up her last sign. It read, *I'm putting hoods over your heads. Walk slowly and follow the boy in front of you.*

Then Sally held up the first sign again, *If you run, you will be shot!*

Sally put a pillowcase over each boy's head and marched them to the van. Each boy was forced into the back of the van. The boys could not see each other or move their hands. Escape was hopeless.

Kimberly drove the van home and parked near the second house. The boys were led downstairs into the basement. Each boy was then led to a cage and placed inside. Kenny was put inside the first cage, then Jake, Tony and Pete.

Sally removed each boy's hood and tossed his sleeping bag and pillow into the cage. Then, Sally locked each cage door. A table sat near one of the cages. On the table were several new signs.

Sally flipped over the first sign. It read, *We will not speak to you. You are prisoners!*

The next sign read, *We may keep you as pets or just kill you. This depends on your ability to follow the rules!*

Rule One - Do not talk to each other or us, ever!

Rule Two - Whenever we enter the building, we will ring a buzzer and you will put your hoods back on!

Rule Three - Behave yourselves always. If you misbehave, you will be beaten or shot!

Rule Four - We may decide to torture one or all of you. If you cry out, we may kill you!

Rule Five - Press the buzzer in your cage if you need to use the bathroom.

Sally picked up the last sign. It read, *Think about the bad things you have done against decent people in the past! Maybe you will survive this, but probably not!*

Tony wanted to speak to the kidnappers and he raised his hand. Sally pointed towards Tony to go ahead and talk.

Tony said, "I need you to know I have asthma and I use an inhaler."

Tony pulled the inhaler from his packet to show Kimberly and Sally.

"My inhaler is about half full. Sometimes I have trouble breathing, especially during stressful situations and I think this would qualify," Tony said while taking a draw on his inhaler.

Sally scribbled something on the back of one of the cardboard signs; it read, *Then maybe you will be even more motivated to follow the rules.*

Tony looked at the sign and could only nod his head in agreement.

Kimberly and Sally left the house, grinning at each other. They were surprised how easy it was to control and snatch four boys, each one stronger than either of them.

Kimberly turned to Sally and said, "The way you handled Tony just now was awesome. Great job!"

Sally managed to smile although she was very stressed out.

The girls went inside the main house, spoke to each other for a few minutes, turned on the microphone located in the barn and went to bed.

Chapter 10

~~~~~~~

Dry White Toast

Sobbing, inside their cages, each boy tried to see each other but they could not. There was some type of a black curtain draped between their cages making it impossible to see the cage next to them. The room was very dark.

Kenny was the first to speak. "Can you guys hear me?"

All four boys, one after each other, replied yes, they could hear him.

Jake said, "Keep your voices down. I don't think these guys are kidding. Those shotguns are real and loaded."

Pete said, "I wonder what we did to piss these assholes off? You can bet our parents will find us."

"Our parents will miss us, and eventually they will call the cops. We were supposed to camp out and come home tomorrow morning," said Tony.

"I don't know how anyone will ever find us. I don't have any idea where we are. For Christ's sake, I don't even know if we are still in Kirtland or not," said Kenny.

"It might take a miracle to find us. We cleared out the campground of our sleeping bags, leftover food and rubbish. There's no proof we actually camped out," said Tony.

"You're both right. We must come up with a plan. Everyone, take a deep breath and try to relax. Lie down and try to get a little sleep. In the morning, maybe the room will be lighter and we will have a better idea how screwed we are," said Kenny.

"I'd say, we're pretty screwed," said Jake.

"Hey Tony," Jake whispered, "You need to relax as much as you can. We don't want to watch you struggle to breathe and not be able to get you help."

"I'll do my best," replied Tony, "But I'm not sure how I can feel relaxed at this point."

Listening to the conversation, Kenny finally spoke up. "Just don't piss them off," said Kenny, "That's all you can do."

Jake crawled into his sleeping bag and attempted to sleep, hoping he might wake up and discover this was all nothing but a nightmare. All the other boys followed suit.

In the morning, the boys realized this was not a dream.

Kenny, lying inside his sleeping bag, wondered what they did wrong. Kenny knew they had never physically hurt anyone during any of their pranks. Sure, they caused some property damage and stole some things, but never harmed anyone. Maybe these thugs captured the wrong kids, and hopefully, they would realize that and release them.

Kenny decided to speak to the boy next to him. "Jake, you awake?" asked Kenny.

"Yeah, I've been up all night. Keep your voice down, I think the others are still sleeping," Jake replied, his voice a muted tone.

Kenny said, "Do you have any idea what we did to these guys?"

"No," replied Jake. "I don't have a clue. Why do you think we are here?"

"All I know is we have to escape," said Kenny. "I'm going batshit being locked up in this cage."

Suddenly, a buzzer sounded in the distance. The boys immediately shut their mouths and put their hoods on over their heads. The boys could hear two distinctive sets of footsteps enter the room.

Kimberly and Sally stopped in front of each cage and opened them one at a time. Both girls wore black clothing and hoods to hide their identities. Kimberly held a loaded shotgun to protect her sister.

Sally reached in to take the boy's hood off while placing a small food tray inside the cage. The meal consisted of a piece of toast, an apple and a glass of water

Once the cage was locked, each boy reached for the glass and drank half the water.

Another sign was turned over. It read, *This glass of water must last you until dinner. Sip it slowly!*

Then, the next sign was turned over. It read, *One of you was talking about escaping? Tell us who was responsible right now, or you will all suffer.*

Bravely, Kenny raised his hand. Then he said to his captors, "You need to tell us what you think we've done. You have the wrong boys. We have never hurt a person in our lives. Let us go!"

There were no more signs to flip over so, in response, Kimberly leveled the handgun with both hands, took aim at Kenny and pulled the trigger. "Click!" This time the chamber was empty.

Kenny was shaking and crying and could only manage to say, "I'm sorry!"

Kimberly and Sally walked out of the basement. Each boy turned to their food and slowly ate the dry, white toast and apple while sipping their water, ever so slowly.

Inside the main home, Kimberly and Sally were laughing aloud.

Kimberly said, "I thought he was going to crap his pants when I pulled the trigger!"

"That was hilarious," said Sally.

Sally continued, "What are we going to do if they do not obey us?"

"We'll have to hurt one of them. There's no other way. We must break these boys down so they obey every rule. Their lives depend on it," said Kimberly.

Sally responded quietly, "Are you really prepared to hurt or kill one of them?"

"I am," said Kimberly without a moment's hesitation.

Kimberly continued, "I'm prepared to kill one or more of them if necessary. I really believe, at some point, we will have to kill all four of them. I'm not going to prison for any of these little bastards!"

Sally lowered her head and said, "I kind of like Pete. Do we have to kill him too?"

Kimberly responded, "Sorry but yes, they all have to die. I was thinking of killing Kenny first, then Tony. That would leave just two, the chubby one and Pete. Controlling two boys would be much easier. You do not have to hurt anyone. I'll take care of it!"

During the day, each boy rang the buzzer to use the restroom. Kimberly and Sally installed a bathroom with a toilet close by. There wasn't a door knob on the door and each boy was limited to only five minutes to use the bathroom. When someone rang the buzzer, they were led to the toilet then back to their cage. Kimberly and Sally wore all black clothing and hoods whenever they entered or left the building.

Later that night, Kimberly and Sally brought dinner to the boys consisting of a grilled cheese sandwich and cup of tomato soup. Each boy quickly ate his food. They were all starving. Jake wondered if his mom was making spaghetti and meatballs. Boy, could he really go for some of that right now. The boys wondered if the police were searching for them.

After dinner, each boy would use the toilet then go back to his cage for the night.

The second day began just like the first day. The boys received breakfast, if you can call it that, which they quickly ate anyway.

Kenny could not help himself. He looked at the taller captor and said, "What did we ever do to you? Let us go. Our parents have to be missing us."

Kimberly motioned to Sally to open the cage. Then Sally put the pillowcase over Kenny's head and marched him out of the basement, and out into the orchard. Kimberly took Sally's handgun and pointed it at Kenny's head. As Sally took Kenny's pillowcase off his head, even she was not prepared for what followed. Kenny, remembering the previous day with the blank round, was not sure what to prepare himself for but he hoped for another empty chamber.

"Both of you, I'm very sorry for whatever I did. Please, please forgive me!" said Kenny.

Boom! Kimberly turned the gun away from Kenny's head and fired the pistol, narrowly missing Kenny.

Kenny fell to the ground, tears rolling from his eyes. Emotionally Kenny said, "Thank you so much, I'm so sorry, I'll be quiet from now on, I promise."

Sally had no words. She was in total disbelief. She was sure Kimberly was going to kill the first boy. Sally and Kimberly marched Kenny back to the basement and into his cage. Both girls were sure Kenny got the message and he would pass it on to the others as soon as they left the room.

Chapter 11

~~~~~~~~

Search Team

In 1963, Kirtland was a township and did not have a police department. The Lake County Sheriff's office patrolled Kirtland, making several passes around the city each day.

On the afternoon of July 6, 1963, the Lake County Sheriff switchboard operator took a call from a frantic parent on Locust Drive in Kirtland. Mrs. Lang told the dispatcher her son Kenny, along with his pals, Jake, Tony, and Pete, did not return home from their overnight camping trip. Normally, according to Mrs. Lang, the boys were always back early after their frequent overnight trips, to check in and do their chores.

Mrs. Lang, along with the other parents, were starting to get worried.

Sheriff's Deputy Coolidge received the radio call regarding the missing boys. He pulled into the Lang driveway around 6:00 pm where he found four sets of parents eagerly waiting for him. Everyone began talking to the Deputy at the same time.

Deputy Coolidge held his hand up to staunch the flow of conversation, "Folks, I know you are worried. Let us take this one step at a time. Please sit down."

Deputy Coolidge asked each parent for the names, ages, and physical description of each missing boy. The parents gave a quick physical description to the deputy then told him the birthdates of each of the boys.

Deputy Coolidge excused himself to radio in the missing boys to his dispatcher. "Four missing boys, Kenny Lang, white male, 5'- 9" tall, weight 150, age 16, Jake Adams, white male, 5'- 8" tall, weight 170, age 15, Tony Sawyer, white male, 5' – 7 tall, weight 140, age 15, Pete Peterson, white male, 5' – 7" tall, weight 130, age 14. Last seen camping out in Gildersleeve Mountain."

The deputy returned to the house to ask the parents if any of them could point him in the direction of the boys' normal campground.

Before the other parents could respond and in tears, Mrs. Sawyer said, "You need to know, our son has asthma and needs to use his inhaler to keep his airways open." Mrs. Sawyer continued, "I'm not sure if Tony left home with a new inhaler or the half-empty one, but any kind of stress can trigger an event. Please find our sons!"

Deputy Coolidge jotted down the information and told Mrs. Sawyer they would do their best to find the boys.

Then, Mr. Sawyer responded to the deputy's original question, "Yes, I might know where they camp. I grew up in the area and I am familiar with the mountains. I can show you where I would go if I were them."

"Alright," replied Deputy Coolidge. "I need everyone else to stay right here. I know you are anxious, but I do not want too many people trampling through the campgrounds disturbing any evidence. I'll let you know if we find anything."

Mr. Sawyer and the deputy drove off down Gildersleeve Drive and towards the mountain, located at the end of the road. Upon arriving, both men hiked up into the mountain looking for the campgrounds.

Mr. Sawyer spotted Table Rock, the place the boys would usually camp. The deputy discovered an old campfire spot, along with some candy bar wrappers. Then, both men hiked down the mountain and back to the patrol car.

The deputy once again radioed his dispatcher, "I need a search team to report to me at the end of Gildersleeve Drive. They should be prepared to hike the mountain, bring along flashlights, water and portable radios, if possible. It is starting to get dark so we need to get a move on this. I will wait right here for the team to arrive. Also, I just learned one of the boys has asthma, and his mother gave me an extra inhaler."

The dispatcher radioed back to let the deputy know the searchers would be arriving soon.

The sheriff thought they might be able to respond faster and cover more ground if they called in the Kirtland Volunteer Fire Department. The dispatcher made the call and within 30 minutes, a dozen volunteers, armed with flashlights and medical supplies arrived at the mountain. Minutes later, the search for the boys began.

Gildersleeve Mountain is well known in the Kirtland area. There are many places on the mountain to camp or hike. Most of the volunteers were very familiar with the landscape. Many of them grew up in the Kirtland area. The men hiked the trails, looked inside the many caves and reported back to the deputy. There were no signs of the boys, only the campfire and some trash. It was unknown if the rubbish belonged to the boys or if the boys were even there the previous evening.

Deputy Coolidge drove Mr. Sawyer back to the Lang home and came inside. The deputy informed the families about locating the old campfire and that volunteers searched the entire area and did not report finding any signs of the boys. The deputy told the parents he would be back in the morning and the police would be thoroughly checking out all the local streets and adjacent areas.

Deputy Coolidge left the house. It was very dark outside. He called his dispatcher to inform the sheriff they could not locate the boys and he asked the sheriff to meet him in Painesville where they could strategize their search.

Arriving at the police station about 30 minutes later, Sheriff Schultz met with Deputy Coolidge and with six of his other deputies. Together they formulated a plan to commence searching at first light the following morning. The deputies, along with other local volunteers, would conduct a door-to-door search of Locust Drive, Gildersleeve Drive, Billings Road, Eagle Road plus the local cemetery grounds.

The following morning, the Lake County Sheriff's Department, along with nearly two dozen volunteers, began their search for the missing boys. All the nearby roads were explored including Chillicothe Road, Route 6 and some of the local farms. One of the farm homes was boarded up, so it was ruled out right away. The sheriff and search party reported at 3:00 pm. They did not find any signs of the missing boys. Sally and Kimberly watched as a volunteer combed through their farm, searching for any sign of the lost boys. One of the deputies rang the doorbell of the main house. Kimberly answered the door. She was polite and accommodating. Kimberly told the deputy they had not seen any boys around the farm. Then she was given a picture of each of the boys to look at. Kimberly reiterated, she was sorry, but she had not seen anyone matching their descriptions.

Back in his cage, Kenny told the boys about his narrow escape. Kenny said, "I honestly thought these bastards were going to kill me. They took off my hood, pointed the gun at my head, then abruptly turned and fired the gun, just missing me." Kenny continued, "We have to be very careful. We cannot ask them any questions and we need to keep our noise down. They seem to hear everything we say."

Jake and the other boys were ecstatic Kenny was all right. Still, they needed to do something, and very soon.

In the morning, Kimberly and Sally brought breakfast to the boys. Each tray contained corn flakes, a cup of milk, a piece of dry white toast and a tall glass of water. Still, the girls did not say a word to the boys. Their silence was killing the boys. They had no idea what to do or say.

Sally brought along a couple of signs. The first sign read, *This gun holds six bullets. There are only two bullets in the gun. Let's see if you are lucky.*

Kimberly aimed the gun at Kenny and pulled the trigger, "Click!"

Then she aimed the gun at Jake and pulled the trigger, "Click!"

Tony was next. At the last second, Kimberly pointed the gun towards the ground and pulled the trigger, "Boom!"

Pete was sure he was about to die. Kimberly pointed her weapon at Pete and pulled the trigger, "Click!"

All four boys began weeping. Still, none of the boys knew why this was happening.

Back at the house, Kimberly was pleased and seemed to gloat because the boys were so afraid.

Sally said to Kimberly, "You seem to be getting a kick out of this."

Kimberly responded, "I am happy. We began this to avenge Daddy. We planned it, arranged it and have executed it perfectly. The police are searching the entire city and they haven't found a clue."

"What are you planning to do with the boys?" asked Sally.

"I haven't decided yet," said Kimberly. "I still think we should kill them, but I don't want to go to prison for any of them. They aren't worth it."

"Why don't we just let them go?" asked Sally.

"If we let them go, they will go directly to the cops and we go to jail," said Kimberly. "Do you want to go to jail?"

"No," replied Sally. "So, what should we do?"

Kimberly responded, "Tomorrow is the fourth day. Let us talk in the morning and come up with a plan. We cannot just let them go. If we do, we must let them go one at a time," Kimberly continued, "Also, we have to take them someplace they won't recognize. Got it?"

"Absolutely," replied Sally. "I couldn't agree more."

Before going to bed, the girls went down to the basement to listen to the boys. Before capturing the boys, Kimberly planted a small microphone located directly over the middle cage then ran the speaker wires back to their home. Kimberly and Sally could hear Jake arguing with Tony and Pete about trying to escape. Jake did not want any part of that. He thought they should just wait it out and maybe they would be released.

Jake asked Tony how his inhaler was holding up and Tony said he only had a couple pulls left. Tony seemed to be very afraid.

Kenny said, "Does anyone have any idea yet who these guys might be or what we did wrong?"

None of the other boys had a clue who these crazy people were and they certainly never thought their captors were females. The thought of that never occurred to any of them.

Kimberly was especially pleased the boys seemed lost and had absolutely no clue it was girls that took them.

Chapter 12

~~~~~~~~

A Line Crossed

The morning of the fourth day began just like the others. The girls made breakfast for the boys, then brought it over to the basement of the house next door.

The usual custom was for Sally to open each cage and leave the food while Kimberly protected her sister with her shotgun. Starting with the first cage, the girls went down the line. First Kenny, then Jake, Pete, and finally Tony. As they entered Tony's cage, they observed he was not moving. Sally tugged back and forth on Tony's shoulder and he still would not move.

Kimberly, thinking this might be some sort of a trick, reared back and kicked Tony, square on the back. Still, there was no movement. Then Kimberly knelt over

Tony and checked his pulse. She could not find a pulse. Both Kimberly and Sally had experience with sick farm animals. They both knew the difference between a sick animal and a dead one. Tony obviously was dead. Sally was extremely upset and began to cry. Kimberly held her finger over her mouth as if to tell Sally to be quiet and not to say anything, then motioned for Sally to follow her outside.

Once the girls left the house, Kimberly held Sally in her arms until she could compose herself. After several minutes of near hysterics, Sally pulled away from her sister.

"What did you do to him?" asked Sally.

"I didn't do anything to him," said Kimberly. "I don't have any idea what happened. Maybe he had an asthma attack. I promise I didn't do anything to him!"

Sally responded, "I don't believe you. You've wanted to kill these boys ever since Daddy died."

Kimberly replied, "Believe what you want. I was not really going to kill any of them. I only wanted to scare the crap out of them. Now we have a big problem. Now, none of the boys can live."

"What the hell are you talking about?" said Sally.

"Well, do you want to let the other three boys go? One is already dead. It doesn't matter why he died, we are ultimately responsible," said Kimberly.

"I don't care!" said Sally. "I want to let the other three boys go. Let us drive them somewhere far away then release them. They don't know they are at our farm," said Sally.

"Let's go back to the basement and remove Tony from his cage. While you are down there, remember not to say a word. I'll drive the van over here and we can put him inside and then take him someplace and hide his body," said Kimberly.

Sally shook her head up and down and the girls went back inside to remove Tony and bring him out the back door. The other boys would not know Tony was even there any longer.

Kimberly drove around the back of the house and together both girls picked up Tony's body and placed him in the back of the van.

Sally was correct. The remaining three boys could not see and were too afraid to ask even a simple question.

Sally and Kimberly drove back to their house and went inside. Kimberly made Sally a cup of hot tea and together they began to toss around ideas about what they should do with Tony.

"You said something some time ago about Lake Erie. What were you thinking?" asked Sally.

Kimberly responded, "You know Daddy has a small fishing boat. We could take the boat out on Lake Erie a few miles, weigh down Tony's body, and drop him in the lake."

"I'm starting to think that might be the best thing to do. We do not have a lot of time so if we do this, we need to act fast," said Sally.

Exhausted and terrified, both girls turned in for the night.

Sally woke the following morning to the smell of bacon frying and hurried down the stairs to find out more about the special occasion.

"What's up?" asked Sally. "You never cook in the morning. It's usually cereal or toast."

Kimberly replied, "Sit down, eat your food then we'll discuss my plan." Kimberly continued, "When you are finished, we will take breakfast to our guests then we can sit down and talk."

"Fine by me," said Sally. "I'm starving."

The sisters sat down at the kitchen table to eat their breakfast, consisting of bacon, and eggs over easy, toast and jelly. Both girls ate quickly. It was after all, a wonderful meal.

Kimberly and Sally brought breakfast to the boys. They also received bacon and scrambled eggs with toast.

Sally turned to Kimberly and asked, "You must have scrambled your brains, and you never feed the boys anything this good. What's going on in that beady little mind of yours?"

Now, back at the main house, Kimberly asked Sally to sit down. Sally was getting anxious to hear about what Kimberly had planned.

"I've been up all night long considering our options regarding Tony. I don't think Lake Erie is a viable option," said Kimberly.

"I thought we had already agreed on this. What changed your mind?" asked Sally.

Kimberly responded, "Well, I think Lake Erie is dangerous for us. First, we need to get the boat hooked up to my van with Tony's body inside and drive to the lake without being seen. Then we need to weigh down his body and drop it in the lake, and we have to make sure his body doesn't pop back up for many years or at all if that's even possible."

"Alright," said Sally. "What do you think we should do? We can't just bury him. That's a sure-fire way to get caught."

"Okay, here goes," said Kimberly. "We own a farm, a ranch where we grow fruit and vegetables. As we plant our crops, we use fertilizer. Let's say, we cut up the body into small pieces, and cover the remains with compost. It would not take long for the remains to decompose and then we can spread it over our crops. It would be virtually impossible to get caught."

"I can see why you didn't tell me this until after breakfast," said Sally. "I think I still might get sick."

"Well, I'm waiting for your idea. If you have a better plan, let's hear it," said Kimberly.

"I don't have a better plan but how do you know the FBI or police wouldn't find some of Tony's remains?" asked Sally.

"What remains?" said Kimberly. "There's nothing left. No body, no blood, no fingerprints, no nothing. Maybe some small bones but we can crush them." Kimberly continued, "Would you rather we feed his body to the hogs?"

"Oh my God! NO!" exclaimed Sally. "By the way, you never refer to Tony by his name. It is always his body or his blood, never Tony's body. Why is that?"

"Sorry, I guess subconsciously I'm trying to remove Tony's name and face from my thoughts," said Kimberly. "We have to do something quickly before the body begins to stink to high heaven."

"Alright," said Sally. "Let's take Tony's body into the barn. I suppose we have to drain the blood before we chop him up, right?"

"That's correct," said Kimberly. "We must prepare him like any other farm animal. We put him on the table, drain the blood, chop him up, and spread him over with compost."

"I suppose we'd better get started," replied Sally. "And he is not just another farm animal."

Kimberly drove the van around to the back of the barn. Both girls removed the body and carried him inside, then placed him on the table.

"Hold up!" exclaimed Sally. "We can't do this."

"Did you come up with a better plan?" asked Kimberly. "What changed?"

Sally responded, "I don't think we need to do anything. We did not kill Tony. He died of an asthma attack or something along those lines. If we desecrate his body, we only look more guilty."

"So, what do we do then?" asked Kimberly.

"Nothing," replied Sally. "Just take Tony's body and drop it off somewhere. We did nothing wrong. How can they trace Tony to us anyways?"

"I see your point. If we chop him up and the cops find even a small piece buried on our land, it looks bad for us. So, where do we take him?" asked Kimberly.

Sally responded, "We drop him off at a place like maybe the Holden Arboretum. There is nobody there at night. We will lay him down on the ground or on a picnic table. They should find him within a couple of hours."

"Do you think we should wash Tony's body off first, to make sure there are no traces of our basement?" asked Sally.

Kimberly shook her head in agreement and said, "That's a great idea. We should probably get started."

The girls quickly washed Tony down. Then, Sally washed his clothes and the back of the van, just to be sure the police could find no evidence to connect Tony to them.

"Let's go back inside the house for now," said Kimberly.

Sally replied, "I have a question for you. You seem to be at peace, almost pleased with what happened to Tony. Is killing someone that easy for you now?"

"Well, like you said, we didn't kill him. Tony died on his own," Kimberly shrugged.

"That's bullshit and you know it," said Sally. "When I went through his pockets, I found an empty inhaler. We should have known he was sick and knowing this, we should have released him if not all of them. That makes us responsible."

"Maybe you are right, I hate what they did to Daddy," said Kimberly. "Do you want to let them go and call the police? Is that what you want?"

"No, let's just do this," replied Sally.

After dinner, the girls decided it was time to move Tony. They dressed him in his clean clothes and placed him in the back of the clean van. Then at dusk, Kimberly and Sally drove off towards a local park.

Kimberly decided to take the back way. She drove down Route 6 to Sperry Road then north to the Holden Arboretum, a beautiful nature and plant reserve with over three thousand acres of land. After dodging some geese and other wildlife, Kimberly found a quiet area with a picnic table. The van was backed up to the picnic table and Kimberly and Sally unloaded Tony and placed him, very carefully, on the top of the table.

On the trip home, neither girl knew how to feel or act. Kimberly said to her sister, "I hope we didn't mess up. Maybe we should have driven Tony further away."

"Perhaps," said Sally. "It's too late now. We need to concentrate on the remaining three boys and what we're going to do with them."

Pulling into their driveway, Kimberly said, "Let's check on our guests and go to bed."

"Sounds good," replied Sally.

Chapter 13

~~~~~~~~

A Sawyer Tragedy

At approximately 8:30 am the following morning, the Lake County Sheriff received an urgent phone call. The body of a boy, apparently deceased, was found by the groundskeeper at the Holden Arboretum. The sheriff immediately dispatched a car to the location.

Deputy Tomlin could immediately tell upon arrival that the body was that of a deceased male so he immediately called for the Lake County Coroner. The deputy gave the body a quick once over. He noticed the boy seemed almost at peace. He did not seem to suffer. There were no apparent bullet or knife wounds or any marks from an apparent strangulation. Deputy Tomlin taped off the entire area and called for backup to keep the local news and public far away from the scene.

Around 9:00 am, the coroner pulled up to the scene. Like the deputy, the coroner checked over the body, looking for obvious signs of murder and or suicide. The boy did not have identification or any money. Based on the initial findings, including body temperature and obvious signs of rigor mortis the coroner called the time of death at somewhere between 10:00 pm and 6:00 am the previous night. Since the outside temperature was in the low 50's, establishing the exact time of death would take some time.

Deputy Coolidge arrived on the scene at 9:00 am. The deputy still had photos from the four missing boys on his person. After comparing the photos of the four missing Kirtland boys, the deputy was positive this body was that of the missing 15-year-old Kirtland boy, Tony Sawyer. Deputy Coolidge then contacted the sheriff for instructions on how to proceed. Deputy Coolidge was sent to the Sawyer home on Locust Drive along with instructions to bring the parents in for a positive identification.

After photographs were taken from every conceivable angle, the body was placed in a zippered body bag and transported to the coroner's office in Painesville for an autopsy.

This autopsy was determined to be of the highest priority. Blood was drawn to check for signs of alcohol or pharmaceuticals. No signs of trauma were found. The boy appeared to be dehydrated. The stomach content contained only small particles of food. Upon finding signs of progressive lung disease, the coroner determined the boy died from an episode of asthma although he could not determine if the death was intentional or accidental.

Many questions needed to be answered. Where was this boy being kept for the past several days? Where did these small puncture wounds come from? Who placed the body on the picnic table? Where are the other three boys?

Mr. and Mrs. Sawyer arrived at the coroner's office around noon. Mrs. Sawyer broke down in tears as her husband positively identified the deceased boy was that of his son Tony Sawyer.

Mr. and Mrs. Sawyer sat down with the deputy and the sheriff later that afternoon. Mr. Sawyer demanded answers. He knew his son could easily handle an asthma attack if he had the proper inhaler. To him, the death was not accidental at all. Someone deprived his son of the inhaler. That could be the only explanation.

By the time Mr. and Mrs. Sawyer returned to their home, the news of their son's death had spread throughout Kirtland. As the Sawyer's pulled into their driveway, they could see Mr. and Mrs. Lang, Mr. and Mrs. Adams and Mr. and Mrs. Peterson waiting for them.

Mrs. Sawyer ran into her house and into her bedroom. She was far too traumatized to deal with the other parents. Politely, Mr. Sawyer spoke briefly with the other parents. He told them about the groundskeeper finding Tony's body and the initial findings of the cause of death. There were far too many questions and far too few answers to satisfy any of the parents, including the Sawyers.

That evening during dinner, the boys were discussing Tony. Pete told the other boys he tried talking to Tony numerous times over the past day but didn't receive any response.

"What do you think is going on?" asked Pete.

Neither Jake nor Kenny had an answer to this question.

"Maybe Tony got sick from his asthma and they took him to the hospital," said Pete.

"Yeah, or maybe they murdered him. That seems more likely to me," said Jake. "When they come back in here, someone needs to ask them about Tony."

Pete replied, "I nominate you Kenny. You are the oldest."

"That's true, but you are the ugliest, so I vote for you," Kenny fired back.

"It's amazing we can keep a sense of humor," said Jake.

"Okay, I'll ask them," said Kenny, "But don't expect them to say anything. They haven't said a word so far, so why start now?"

"Shhhhh, I hear someone coming in," said Jake.

As the kidnappers came into Kenny's view, he promptly began asking questions.

"Where's Tony? Is he even here or is he dead?" asked Kenny. Both the girls just stared at Kenny and they did not say a word in response.

Kenny was starting to get agitated now. "I said where the hell is Tony? What did you do to him?" asked Kenny.

Kimberly stared back at Kenny and placed her finger over her lips, as if to tell him to be quiet.

"That's not going to work anymore asshole. Where's Tony?" Kenny shouted.

Kimberly walked over to the spigot and turned the hose on high. Then she brought the hose over in front of each cage and blasted each of them with cold water. Again, Kimberly placed her finger over her lips.

Kenny held up his middle finger in response but dared not say anything else.

After the girls left the basement, Kenny said to the other boys, "Look, if Tony is dead…and I think he is, these animals are going to kill us too. We have to come up with a plan. A plan to escape."

"Jesus, shut the fuck up," said Jake. "What if they can hear us?"

"Do you want to die in here?" asked Kenny.

"No," replied Jake, "But we have to be very careful. They have the keys and the guns. We do not have a clue where we are. So, what's your plan?"

Unexpectedly, the girls came back into the room and they began poking Jake and the other boys with sharp sticks.

Kimberly again held her index finger to her lips. Nobody dared to say a word or hold up his middle finger.

All three boys were bloody from various puncture wounds.

When Kenny thought they were probably alone, he said to the other boys, "I'm sick of this shit. When they feed us tomorrow morning, I'm going to take off."

"Just be careful dumbass," said Jake.

"If you get away, run your ass off. You have a better chance of getting away than we do," said Pete.

"Here's my plan. As soon as one of these buttheads opens the cage, you guys start rattling your cages and yelling. Both of those assholes might briefly look away from me. Once they do, I'll push past them and run like my life depends on it," said Kenny.

Pete responded, "What if they get pissed and try to kill us?"

"I agree with Kenny," said Jake. "We have to try something, or we might die in these cages."

Back at the house, the girls slowly ate dinner. Finally, Kimberly looked at Sally and said, "We need to decide what to do with the others."

Sally shuddered at the thought of what her sister had in mind.

Chapter 14

~~~~~~~

Escape Plan

All three boys spent a very restless night in the barn. None of them had any idea what to expect when Kenny attempted his escape, but the boys took turns wishing him luck.

They were sure Tony was dead. What other explanation could there be? Surely, the kidnappers did not release Tony. If they had, the police would have saved the others by now.

Kenny knew the time to escape was approaching fast. He went over the plan in his mind repeatedly. If he could just push one of the captors aside long enough for him to make his break, he might be able to outrun both. Then again, Kenny did not know where they were or how far he would have to run. He did not even know what direction to run, but he had to try.

Kenny could hear the basement door opening. As usual, one of the offenders carried the food and the other held a pistol.

Per the plan, just as Sally opened the cage door and leaned over to lay the food tray down, Pete and Jake began screaming and shaking their cages. Kimberly took a couple of steps toward the boys then pointed her gun at each boy.

Suddenly, Kenny pushed past Sally and he bolted up the steps. For the first time in over a week, Kenny could see daylight. As soon as Kenny stepped outside, he knew exactly where he was. He had been at this farm many times before. Kenny began sprinting towards the woods and eventual safety.

Kimberly ran up the stairs after Kenny. Kimberly spotted the boy and she noted to herself how fast he was. Then she pointed her pistol and fired once. Kenny kept running. Calmly, Kimberly fired a second time, instantly dropping Kenny in his tracks. Then Kimberly slowly walked towards Kenny and looked over his injured body. Both bullets had hit Kenny, but the first wound was not critical and had little effect on him.

Kenny was lying on his back, struggling in obvious pain, and his breathing was labored. Kimberly could see the blood gushing from the second wound. The second bullet hit Kenny on the neck. He was losing a lot of blood. Kimberly leered down at Kenny, aimed the gun towards his head, and pulled the trigger for the final time.

Almost giddy, Kimberly strolled back to the barn and went inside. The girls were still not speaking in front of their captives, so Kimberly took Sally by the arm and marched her outside.

Once outside, Sally could see Kenny lying motionlessly in the orchard.

"Jesus," said Sally. "What did you do that for?"

"Because he was going to get away," replied Kimberly. "If he did escape, the police would be here by now and we'd be going to jail. I could not catch him because he was too fast. Shooting him was my only option."

Sally responded, "I can't think straight. This is wrong. What can we do with Kenny's body?"

"We have to think of a good way to flush this turd," said Kimberly.

"His name was Kenny," said Sally. "He was a human being for Christ's sake. Say his name, Kenny."

"Fine," replied Kimberly. "His name is Kenny. Now, let's have breakfast and think about what to do with Kenny."

"How can you think about food? Are we going to bother to feed the other two?" asked Sally.

"No, they lost their food privileges for today," answered Kimberly.

After breakfast, Kimberly and Sally sat down on the sofa to discuss their next move.

"Maybe we can chop him up or bury him on our land," said Kimberly.

"I disagree," replied Sally. "His body can never be discovered. What are the other options? Can we drop Kenny into Lake Erie without getting caught?"

"It's possible," said Kimberly. "First, I think we need to remove both empty cages. Then, when it is dark out, we can disassemble the cages and bring the parts to our boat. Then take the boat to Mentor and drop everything in the lake."

"Why do we need to remove the cages?" asked Sally.

"Just a precaution. We need to get rid of as much evidence as possible. If we ever get caught, we better not have any cages or their sleeping bags or any other personal items," replied Kimberly.

Sally agreed to the new plan and both girls went into the basement to remove the cages. Kenny's cage was removed from the front of the house and Tony's from the back of the house. Kimberly figured this way the remaining boys could not see what they were doing.

Kimberly began to disassemble one of the cages and Sally took the other one apart. It only took an hour before the sides, tops, and bottoms of each cage were sitting inside the van, waiting for transport to the lake.

"I have an idea," said Sally.

"At this point, I'm open to all ideas," said Kimberly.

"Alright, here it goes. What if we sandwich Kenny's body between two of the cage sides? Then we could fasten the cages together with wire and drop him in the lake. I think the steel from the cages would weigh Kenny down," said Sally.

"Sounds like a plan. First, I need to do one thing," said Kimberly.

"What's that?" asked Sally.

"I read somewhere we have to cut Kenny open and remove his innards or his body will bloat and rise to the surface. That would be bad for us," said Kimberly.

"Jesus," said Sally. "What have we become?"

"I'm only kidding," replied Kimberly. "But I'd say we have become vindictive bitches. Also, don't forget, we were put into this position by these boys. They are responsible for our father's fatal heart attack."

"I know," replied Sally.

Then Kimberly said, "I like your idea of using the cage sides. I think we should cut them in half, right down the middle. Then we wait until the middle of the night when the lake is less populated and then sandwich his body between two smaller pieces, instead of the massive sides. The pieces would be easier to transport to and from the boat."

"That sounds fine," said Sally. "I'll take one of the torches and you take the other. We'll cut these cage pieces in half."

Kimberly and Sally's father taught them everything about the farm and farm equipment. Sally lit the torch like a pro and expertly cut the sides of her cage in half. The steel cut like butter. Both Kimberly and Sally finished at the same time.

Then, Kimberly backed the van up into the barn and both girls carried the body to the van. Previously deciding not to drain Kenny's body, Kimberly wrapped him in plastic so blood would not get all over her van.

Kimberly and Sally placed Kenny's body between two partial cages and fastened the sides together using wire, normally used to mend fences. The heavy-duty stainless-steel wire would not rust and should remain intact for years to come. Then, all the cage pieces along with Kenny's body were placed into the van. Kimberly attached their boat trailer to the van, and the girls were ready for the sun to set.

During the summer months, the sun did not set until later in the evening. After dinner, Kimberly and Sally brought some food to their two remaining boarders.

"I thought you weren't going to feed the boys today," said Sally.

"I changed my mind," replied Kimberly. "I don't think they are going to be with us for much longer."

"What's that supposed to mean?" asked Sally.

"You know exactly what this means," said Kimberly. "We have to kill them, all of them or should I say, the last of them."

Kimberly stared at Sally then calmly said, "Do you understand why they have to die? We cannot have any witnesses. I hope you get that."

Sally responded, "Yes, I understand. That doesn't mean I agree."

Chapter 15

~~~~~~

Unholy Burial

Jake and Pete ate their dinner slowly. Both boys were thinking the same thing.

Jake was the first to speak. "Do you think we are going to die?" asked Jake.

"Yeah, I think so. These people are nuts. I think, for some reason, they want to kill us. I don't know what we did to them, but they hate us and want us dead," replied Pete.

"Do you think we should try to escape as Kenny did?" asked Jake.

"I don't think we have any choice," said Pete. "What if we take our food tray and break it into pieces.

Then maybe we can find a sharp piece we can attack them with."

"It's worth a try," said Jake. "I don't want to die in this shithole. I miss my family and I want to see them again." Jake began sobbing uncontrollably. He was beyond afraid yet wanted to at least try to escape.

Pete began pulling and twisting his plastic tray. After several minutes of strenuous determination, the tray snapped, leaving fragments all over the bottom of the cage, including several very sharp pieces. Jake did the exact same thing. Now, both boys were armed.

"You'll have to stab the person holding the gun right in the throat," said Pete. "I mean jam it in as hard as you can. If you can get the gun, try to shoot them both. If they open my door first, I will try to do the same thing. All right? Now hide those broken pieces under your sleeping bag and try to get some rest."

"Just so we agree, if they come for the tray tonight or in the morning, we attack them, right?" asked Jake.

"Yes, if they show up tonight, we do it, if not we make our move in the morning," said Pete. "You will see your family again, I promise."

The sun was starting to set as Kimberly and Sally pulled into the unloading area at Mentor on the lake. Kimberly backed the trailer a few feet out into the lake and stopped the van.

"As soon as we open the back door of the van, we'll need to act quickly," said Kimberly. "After we disconnect the boat from the trailer, you hop in the boat, start it up, and wait for me."

"I've never started up or driven the boat," Sally replied nervously.

"Well, there's no better time to learn than right now," said Kimberly. "I'll walk you through it."

"Sounds good to me," replied Sally.

Kimberly unhooked the boat from the trailer and cranked the boat into the lake. Then, Sally hopped into the boat and with minimal effort, started the motor.

"I knew you could do it," said Kimberly.

Suddenly, Kimberly spotted another boat arrive at the dock.

Terrified, both girls watched as a pickup truck backed a trailer down the ramp, alongside Kimberly and Sally. A man flew out of the cab and approached the girls.

"Do you ladies need any help?" asked the man.

"No, sir," replied Kimberly. "I'm teaching my sister how to take the boat off and on the trailer. It's always best to learn when the boat ramp is deserted."

"Absolutely," replied the man. "If you need anything just let me know."

Sally stood next to the man as he expertly slid his boat off the trailer and into the lake. Shortly afterward, he started the boat and drove off while a second man drove the trailer up to the parking lot.

"Sally, did you see how they did it?" asked Kimberly.

"Yup," replied Sally. "Doesn't look too difficult."

"Alright, as soon as both men get into their boat and drive off, we'll unload our cargo and you'll take off. I'll park the car and meet you at the end of the dock," said Kimberly.

As the second man jumped into their boat and they headed out, Kimberly scanned the landscape for other potential witnesses.

With nobody in sight, Kimberly unlocked the back of the van. Between the weight of the young boy and the cages, the girls struggled to handle the cargo. However, they eventually managed to secure their freight.

Sally pulled their boat towards the end of the dock while Kimberly parked the van and trailer.

Kimberly sprinted back towards the end of the dock and jumped into the boat. Taking control of the throttle, Kimberly sped off.

"I think chopping him up and making fertilizer out of him might have been easier," said Kimberly.

"Please, let's just get this over with. I am a nervous wreck. I keep looking over my shoulder expecting to see the blue lights of the police in the background at any moment," replied Sally.

Kimberly stopped the boat about five miles out and scanned the area for any witnesses. Seeing nobody around, Kimberly decided this would be a great place to drop their load. Sally and Kimberly grabbed both ends of the cage and tossed Kenny overboard. The cage, along with Kenny's body, quickly sank into the murky waters of Lake Erie.

Chapter 16

The Remaining Boys

The ride back to Kirtland was unusually quiet for Kimberly and Sally. Neither girl had much to say.

Sally was first to break the ice. "So, what are we going to do with Jake and Pete?" asked Sally.

"Well, we can't just pretend they aren't here. They have to go away, far away," replied Kimberly.

"When are you planning to deal with them?" asked Sally.

Kimberly replied, "I was considering shooting both boys tomorrow. Are you alright with that?"

Learning not to challenge her sister, Sally replied that she just wanted to get it over with.

Kimberly said, "Alright, tomorrow it is."

"I'm not sure who you are anymore," Sally said to her sister. "You are starting to frighten me."

"I'm sorry you feel that way," replied Kimberly. "I'm just focused on doing what we have to do and getting rid of the evidence. I don't want to go to jail either."

By the time the girls pulled into the driveway, they were exhausted. After dinner, Sally sat down with her sister to talk about Jake and Pete.

"Look," said Sally. "I don't think we should kill them. Killing one was plenty. I think we need to let them go."

"Why on earth would I ever agree to that?" asked Kimberly.

"What if we drive them to Cleveland or Columbus and let them go?" said Sally. "They didn't see us. They do not know where they are and they have not heard our voices," said Sally.

"That's for sure," said Kimberly. "What if we remove them from their cages, tie them up, then drive them someplace far away and drop them off? That would give us time to destroy the cages and clean up the basement."

"I like that idea," replied Sally.

"Okay, it's a plan," said Kimberly. "I just hope it works or our asses are in a big sling. We should get busy and do it right now."

"Alright by me," said Sally. "Let's find some rope to tie them up with. Remember they have to wear their hoods the entire time and we cannot speak."

Kimberly and Sally quickly found some twine and rope in the barn and went down into the basement to tie Pete and Jake up.

As usual, Kimberly held a gun on the boys. Sally brought along several cardboard signs for Jake and Pete to read.

The first sign read, *We are going to drive you some place and release you. We will tie you up and put you in the van.*

The second sign read, *If you fight us, you will be shot.*

The final sign read, *You must wear your hoods at all times, starting now.*

Not knowing what else to do, Pete and Jake put their hoods on. One at a time, each cage was opened then both boys were tied up and placed in the van.

Kimberly stood watch as Sally took the torch and cut up both cages.

"I hope we're doing the right thing," said Kimberly.

"I'm scared too," replied Sally.

After cleaning the basement, Kimberly walked towards Sally. Upon reaching her, Kimberly held out her arms and pulled her sister in to embrace her. Neither girl wanted to let the other go.

"Sally, like I told you before. None of this was your idea. If the police come, and they might, remember you did not kill anyone and you deny doing anything wrong," said Kimberly. "Also, and this is important, when they talk to you, refuse to answer any questions and ask for a lawyer."

"I won't tell them a damn thing," said Sally. "They have no evidence, no motive, therefore no crime," replied Sally. "They'll have to torture me before I say anything."

Kimberly laughed for the first time in a week. "Let's hope it won't come to that," said Kimberly. "Now remember, they might say stuff to you such as Kimberly told us everything or Kimberly blamed you for kidnapping the boys."

Kimberly continued, "When they say things like this, just remember I will never tell them a thing. I will deny all charges. The boys never saw our faces or heard us talk. Besides, they think we are men."

Sally responded, "Alright, I promise they won't hear anything from me. Now, what do we need to do?"

Kimberly began, "First, we need to burn the sleeping bags, sharpened sticks, and gloves. Also, we need to bring along our guns and ammo. Then we need to clean the barn with soap, water, and bleach. We can take turns. One of us always needs to guard the boys. After we burn all the evidence, we can drop off the boys, then afterwards we toss the cage pieces, guns and bullets into the Chagrin River.

Sally stood very still. Up to now, she really had no understanding of what freeing the boys would mean. She hoped the boys would go home and nobody would ever come looking for them. But things would only get more complicated.

Chapter 17

~~~~~~~

Jake and Pete

The bonfire at the Roberts' farm was dying off. The sleeping bags burned quickly. Adding a little gasoline to the fire helped immensely. Now it was time to drive the boys somewhere safe. The idea was to drop them off and still have enough time to get back home, just to make sure everything was taken care of.

Before getting into the van, Sally asked her sister, "So where should we take them?"

"I've been thinking about that," said Kimberly. "I have a couple of ideas. What about Edgewater Park in Cleveland? We could drive to the back of the park and drop them off. Or there's the Cleveland Zoo."

"Edgewater Park works for me. Do you remember the place where we watched fireworks a couple of years ago with Daddy?" asked Sally.

"Yes, I do," replied Kimberly. "Once we get into the van, we cannot speak to each other. After we find a good place to drop the boys off, we need to cover our license plate with this cardboard before leaving."

"I'm ready," said Sally.

The girls began the trip from Kirtland to Edgewater Park on the west side of Cleveland. Both girls had been there with their father many times before. As they passed the Cleveland Indian Stadium and giant Chief Wahoo sign near the 9th Street Pier, the girls began getting nervous. Kimberly was not at all sure they were doing the right thing.

The van entered the park and drove to the far side overlooking Lake Erie. The evening view with the lights from all the boats and the stars in the sky was spectacular.

Kimberly stopped the van and they waited a few minutes until they were sure nobody was around. Then both girls exited the van. Sally taped a small piece of cardboard over the license plate while Kimberly took the boys out of the back. Kimberly forced each boy to sit down on the grass while she quickly drove away from the scene.

Jake and Pete were not sure if they were free or if they were about to be killed. Hesitantly, Jake removed his hood. Jake looked around to get his bearings but did not recognize any scenery. Then Jake helped Pete take off his hood.

Both boys sat there, wondering if their ordeal was over or if the kidnappers might return. The boys chose to move to a different location just in case their captors decided to return. A few minutes later, Jake and Pete began looking for help.

Jake and Pete decided to walk down a dirt pathway. Several minutes later, they came across a couple walking through the park. Jake briefly told the couple about their ordeal and asked if they could untie them. The man and his wife were horrified hearing about what the boys had just gone through. They untied the boys and drove them over to Captain Franks, a popular Cleveland restaurant, and called the police. The restaurant gave both boys a Coca-Cola while they waited for the police to arrive.

The Cleveland Police arrived quickly and began asking the boys for more information. Jake told Officer King their names and addresses and they were from Kirtland and were kidnapped at gunpoint a week or so earlier. The police seemed apprehensive after hearing this tall tale, but the officer went out to his patrol car to call in the report. Seconds later, the dispatcher validated the report of teenage boys missing from the Kirtland area. If the boys were found, the orders were to immediately notify the Lake County sheriff. Officer King went back inside the restaurant to take written statements from the couple that rescued the boys. Then, the officer collected the boy's hoods and bindings into evidence.

The Cleveland police dispatcher called the Lake County sheriff, who in turn notified the FBI and the Adams and Peterson families. The Cleveland police drove Jake and Pete to the Euclid General Hospital where they were met by the sheriff and their parents. The reunion was extraordinary. Neither Mrs. Adams nor Mrs. Peterson wanted to let their sons go.

The police asked the parents for a few minutes alone with their sons. The boys' mothers were reluctant, but their fathers understood the police needed to do their jobs, so they agreed. Once alone, the sheriff's deputy began asking for information about the kidnapping, in detail. The police informed Jake and Pete about finding Tony's body. Both boys cried after hearing about Tony. But the police officers did not have any idea what caused his death and they asked the boys if they could assist by adding any details. The main question on the minds of the officers was what happened to Kenny Lang.

Jake and Pete both told the police the story about sleeping out at Gildersleeve Mountain when two men kidnapped them at gunpoint. Their abductors never spoke and they never saw their faces. They told the police about the signs the kidnappers forced them to read with their rules. Whenever encountering each other, either the boys wore hoods or the kidnappers wore a mask. Also, the boys could not see each other so they did not know what happened to Tony. They tried calling out for him, but they did not know he was dead. Pete did remember hearing Tony struggling to breathe, but he did not say anything. Pete thought Tony was trying to protect the other boys, so maybe that was why he never called for help.

Then Jake told the police about their last conversation with Kenny. He had decided to break free in the morning as their captors served breakfast. Jake told them about the two boys shaking their cages and screaming to distract the kidnappers to give Kenny a chance to escape. Then they described hearing two or three gunshots, and neither Jake nor Pete ever saw or heard from Kenny again. They assumed he was murdered.

The doctor who treated both boys at the hospital recommended that they stay overnight for observation. Both boys appeared to be dehydrated so intravenous fluids were ordered and each boy received a hot meal from the cafeteria.

The sheriff's deputy signed a chain of custody for the ropes and hoods, then the Cleveland police wished the boys and their parents well. Both boys hugged Officer King and their parents vigorously shook his hand.

Chapter 18

Case Heating Up

Kimberly and Sally went back to their normal routine. Kimberly telephoned their farm hands to ask them to return. To make sure they did not leave any evidence or any signs the boys had ever been there, Kimberly and Sally went over the property, repeatedly. Sally was particularly anxious about their involvement being discovered. Every time she heard a siren or a strange noise, she wondered if the authorities were coming for them.

With autumn fast approaching, Kimberly decided to take Sally shopping for school clothes and supplies. Kimberly anticipated this shopping trip might take Sally's mind off her anxieties.

Kimberly drove to the Great Lakes Mall to shop at JC Penney. The girls found a great selection of tops and skirts for young ladies. Before long, Sally had an entirely new wardrobe for school.

Kimberly also took Sally to Newberry's to purchase school supplies such as pens, pencils, and notebooks. After they finished shopping, the girls sat at Newberry's coffee shop for ice cream. Both girls had a wonderful time and thankfully the trip did help take their mind off things.

Back on Locust Drive, Jake and Pete were home, but they were struggling over their recent ordeal. The boys went over their history of pranking people to see if anything they did rose to the level of someone kidnapping and possibly murdering them. They could not think of a thing. Jake knew the boys stole a few things and put some dog crap into the telephone change returns plus had a car towed. The meanest thing they could remember doing was flipping an apple and breaking a back window or destroying some apples and watermelons at the farmer's lot. In all these instances, the boys were never caught. Nobody ever found out who they were.

Jake and Pete wanted to sit down with both Kenny's and Tony's parents. Although Jake's parents did not think this was a good idea, they agreed to take the boys over for a visit.

During the visit, Jake and Pete tried to tell the other parents about their ordeal. Jake had to choke back tears several times as he relayed instances of when they were being held captive. He was not sure if talking about this would help or hurt the other parents. Jake only thought they should hear first-hand what they went through.

For the first week or so after their release, the police called every day. Soon, they were calling every other day, then maybe once a week. The police did not have any clues other than the hoods the boys were forced to wear and ropes they were tied with. The parents of all four boys called the sheriff and demanded a meeting with the police, FBI, and district attorney. They wanted answers.

The sheriff decided to hold the meeting although he felt, because of the lack of evidence, it would be rather counterproductive. Still, he arranged and attended the meeting.

The meeting began politely. The sheriff soon turned the meeting over to the district attorney, Mr. Coletti.

Mr. Coletti was the Lake County District Attorney for almost ten years. When he said, "This is what we know so far," everyone began paying close attention. Then Mr. Coletti went on to say, "We ask you to keep this information to those in this room only. Does everyone agree?"

Mr. Coletti said to the group, "Alright, first thanks for coming in tonight. We understand you are all upset and you wonder if the case is going cold. First, let me assure you, the case is not cold. It is beginning to heat up. It's only been a couple of weeks and for this type of investigation, it usually takes much longer to have any sort of progress."

Mr. Coletti continued, "With regards to Tony. The autopsy revealed his lungs were closed off due to an extreme asthma attack. Since we know stressful situations can trigger an asthma attack, and we know Tony was under stress, the kidnappers are responsible for his stress and therefore his eventual death. We consider the crimes against Tony to be felony kidnapping, false imprisonment, torture and manslaughter. If we convict on these charges, the perpetrators could receive a life sentence, just for crimes against Tony alone."

Mr. Sawyer thanked the district attorney for his update.

Mr. Coletti replied, "Regarding Jake and Pete, these criminals could face a life sentence for felony kidnapping, torture, and false imprisonment. We will prosecute these men to the fullest extent of the law."

Mr. Coletti continued, "Now regarding Kenny Lang. We know he was kidnapped, tortured, and imprisoned along with the rest of the boys. These men will face the same charges as Jake and Pete. However, we do not know what happened to Kenny. As much as I hate to say this, Kenny was likely murdered. We do not know exactly what they did to him or where his remains are. If we can find Kenny's remains and those responsible for his probable death, we may seek the death penalty. Until we know more about what happened to Kenny, the responsible people will not be charged. This is our ace in the hole."

"Thanks for your update," replied Mr. Lang. "Now, the question we all want answered is, can you catch them?"

"At this time, I'd like to hand this meeting over to the FBI. Let me introduce you to Agent Brian Wilhelm from the FBI," said Mr. Coletti.

"We know you are anxious and you deserve justice for your sons. I cannot go into a lot of detail, however, we do have suspects, two men from East Cleveland," said Agent Wilhelm.

"That's outstanding," replied Mrs. Adams. "Can you tell us anything else?"

"I will say this, we are investigating two Cleveland men. Both men have convictions for kidnapping in their past. They served most of their sentence and got out of prison two years ago," responded Agent Wilhelm. "Now, these crimes and their past crimes are not the same. Previously, they demanded a ransom. That is not the case here. Also, the men who took your children never spoke to them. Previously, they spoke with their prisoners and never hid their faces," said Agent Wilhelm.

"Thanks very much for this information," said Mrs. Sawyer.

With the meeting concluded, the parents left the building with a slim glimmer of hope they would get justice for their boys.

The sheriff, Agent Wilhelm, and Mr. Coletti remained in the office.

Mr. Coletti began the discussion. "Seriously, we have to give these families some closure. I can't even imagine how difficult this is for them," said Mr. Coletti.

Mr. Coletti continued, "We plan to interview the two suspects this week. I expect them to cooperate, but you never know. I will keep you posted on how things are going. These men better have a good alibi, or they are in deep shit. Unless the electric chair is ruled unconstitutional, I will personally throw the switch on these bastards."

Chapter 19

~~~~~~~~

Suspects

Jake spent the last weeks of summer vacation alone in his house. He refused to go outside unless he was in the presence of an adult. Jake was shaken to the core. Pete was doing slightly better than Jake. Although Pete did not go anywhere alone, his mom took the time to drive Pete over to Jake's house so that they could spend time together.

Jake had very little appetite. At dinner, he spent most of the time pushing the food around his plate. Jake's parents were very concerned, but they did not know how to help him. Mr. and Mrs. Adams considered finding a therapist to help Jake through his ordeal.

Jake and Pete's lives were completely changed, and they were not even sure why. For both boys, the pranks were over. Stealing fruit was over, and camping out was never going to happen again.

The first week after Labor Day, school began as usual. Jake was a junior and Pete a sophomore, the same as Sally Roberts.

Pete was looking forward to going back to school. He wanted to see if he could get Sally to go out with him.

Jake only wanted to be left alone. Jake's mom tried talking to him about the ordeal, but Jake shut everyone out. Jake considered dropping out of school, but his father would never allow that to happen. Mr. Adams was a stickler for getting a solid education. He told Jake that he would not only finish high school but he would also attend college. Jake did not handle the pressure well, but he decided he would go back to school and dive into the books.

Life on the Roberts' farm was business as usual. The girls and their farmhands were preparing for the fall harvest. Before the farmhands returned, Kimberly replaced the door knob into the bathroom. With nothing out of the ordinary, neither farmhand suspected a thing.

Kimberly and Sally spent many hours discussing the summer's events. Kimberly wanted more than anything to help Sally cope with her role in the kidnapping and deaths of two of the boys. Kimberly took on almost a motherly role. She spoke to Sally often and hugged her every chance she got. It seemed to Sally that Kimberly was really regretting the whole fiasco.

"Is there anything else you need for school?" Kimberly asked Sally.

"No," replied Sally.

"What's the matter?" asked Kimberly.

"To tell you the truth, I don't want to go back to school at all. I just want to drop out," replied Sally.

"I don't have to tell you, Daddy wouldn't want you to drop out of school," said Kimberly.

"I'm pretty sure Daddy wouldn't want us to be involved with the death of two boys either," said Sally. "But here we are."

"I understand," replied Kimberly. "I'll make you a deal. You go back to school and if you feel the same way after a couple of weeks, you can drop out."

Kimberly continued, "You are 16 years old now so you can legally drop out. I'd love to attend your graduation, though."

"Yeah, maybe you can attend from prison," replied Sally.

"As I told you many times, you will never be held responsible. I will shoulder the entire blame if it comes to that," said Kimberly.

"I'm sorry," replied Sally. "Maybe I just need to get back to a routine. I will do as you ask," said Sally.

Kimberly responded, "Great, just keep talking to me when you are feeling down. Don't carry the blame. The blame falls on my shoulders and mine alone."

"Thanks for saying that. I appreciate it, but I was there, every step of the way," Sally replied morosely as she walked out of the room.

This was also a busy time at the FBI field office in Cleveland. Agent Wilhelm was looking to bring in two Columbus men for an interview. The two men, recently released from the Ohio State Penitentiary near Columbus, Ohio, completed eight years out of a ten-year sentence for a 1952 kidnapping of a young boy and holding him for a $5,000 ransom.

Eventually, the child was released unharmed and both men surrendered to the authorities, without collecting on the ransom. At the time, there was public outrage because of the relatively short sentence.

Following up on a lead, Agent Wilhelm was able to locate the men and brought them to Cleveland for the interview. Initially, both men refused to take a polygraph, something they learned from their time in prison. To Agent Wilhelm and other agents, the refusal to take the polygraph was an indicator of their guilt. Refusing this test allowed the FBI to turn up the heat.

The two men were separated. It was evident that one man, Teddy Bowman, was criminally sophisticated and the FBI did not think he would crack under pressure. However, the other man, Franklin Casey, appeared to be more susceptible to the FBI tactics, so they pounced on him.

Both interviews began easily at first. The men were asked where they were living for the past three years. Teddy Bowman refused to answer. Then, Agent Wilhelm got a little rough. Bowman finally confessed he was living with his friend in Chesterland. The agents discovered Bowman worked at a local hardware store.

This was a red flag because the FBI found Jake and Pete were both tied with rope. When the agent checked out Bowman's employment history, they discovered he was on vacation at the time of the Kirtland kidnappings. The agents considered this a gigantic red flag. Also, he lived in an old home with several acres of land. In other words, Bowman had the means and the time to pull off this kidnapping.

Although Bowman denied even knowing where Kirtland was, Agent Wilhelm did not believe him. Bowman was held without charges while the FBI and Lake County sheriff obtained proper warrants to check out Bowman's home, land, and workplace.

The FBI went hard after Franklin Casey. They quickly found out that Casey was unemployed and living with his pal Bowman at the time of the kidnappings. As with Bowman, Casey had no alibi. He did admit knowing where Kirtland was although he denied kidnapping the four boys and strongly denied killing anyone. Now, Casey told the agents he would consent to a polygraph. The FBI wasted little time. Before Casey knew what was going on, he was strapped into the polygraph machine.

"Is your name Franklin Casey?"

"Yes."

"Do you live in Chesterland, Ohio?"

"Yes."

"Do you live with Teddy Bowman?"

"Yes."

"Do know where the Gildersleeve Mountains are?"

"No."

"Do know where Locust Drive is?"

"No."

"Were you in Kirtland in June of this year?"

"No."

"Have you ever killed anyone?"

"No."

"Did you help kidnap four Kirtland boys?"

"No."

"Did you help torture any of the boys?"

Unresponsive.

"Did you help torture any of the boys?"

"No."

"Did you help kill any of the four boys?"

"I don't think so."

"Please answer the question with a yes or a no."

"Did you help kill any of the four boys?"

"No."

"Do you have a black jacket, black hood or mask and black pants?"

"Yes."

"Did you help place a dead boy on a picnic table?"

"No."

"Did you ever speak to the Kirtland boys?"

"No."

"Did you communicate with the boys using signs?"

"Yes." (I think you meant to say no here)

"Are you sexually attracted to boys?"

"No."

"Did you help release two boys in Cleveland?"

"Yes." (I think you meant to say no here)

"Did you help to kill any of the boys?"

"No."

"Did you help kidnap four Kirtland boys from Gildersleeve Mountains?"

"I do not know what you want from me."

Franklin Casey stood up and ripped off the lie detector wires. The agents slammed him back down in the chair. Casey began to cry and asked to talk with his friend. Agent Wilhelm entered the room.

"Let me make this easy for you, Mr. Casey. You failed the polygraph, miserably. I do not even know why you bothered to take it. Let's go over the results, shall we?" said Agent Wilhelm.

You do know where both Locust Drive and the Gildersleeve Mountains are. You have recently kidnapped children. You have murdered somebody in the past, and you are attracted to boys. Do you know what this makes you?

"No," said Franklin Casey.

"Guilty," responded Agent Wilhelm. "Guilty of four counts of felony kidnapping, two counts of aggravated murder, unlawful imprisonment, torture, and molestation of a minor."

"I never molested anyone!" screamed Casey.

"What did you do to them?" asked Wilhelm.

"I just helped Bowman take them but I never touched anyone," said Casey.

The FBI was certain that none of the boys were molested, but they just wanted to get a rise out of Casey.

Casey started crying like a baby. The FBI decided it was time to go for the kill.

Chapter 20

Weakest Link

Before taking the statement, the FBI called the Lake County sheriff and district attorney to let them know they were about to hear the confession from Franklin Casey. Both men were asked to join the FBI and both agreed. The sheriff and DA would be there within the hour. Franklin Casey was brought in dinner and given a chance to relax for a few minutes.

Meanwhile, FBI Agent Mills was asked to speak to the other defendant, Teddy Bowman, who was brought to the interrogation room.

"Teddy, it's only fair to let you know, your pal Casey folded like a cheap suit," said Mills. "He is singing a song right now. A song about your involvement in the kidnapping of four boys from Kirtland and the murder of two of them. You should know, the person who sings the loudest and is the most believable will get a deal and the other will die horribly in the state of Ohio electric chair." Mills continued, "Does that sound like fun to you?"

"First of all, the capital punishment in Ohio is about to be repealed, so you don't scare me," said Bowman. "Secondly, prison isn't so bad, three meals and a warm bed every day, and I don't have to worry about paying rent or buying food. So, go screw yourself!"

"We'll see how smart you are when your partner gives us his statement implicating you in felony kidnapping and murder," said Agent Mills. As Bowman was brought back to the holding cell, Agent Mills smiled to himself. He thought Casey's statement should be very entertaining.

The Lake County sheriff and district attorney entered the FBI field office and were brought back to the interrogation room where Franklin Casey waited along with two FBI agents. Agent Wilhelm shared the polygraph report administered to Casey. Although the test revealed some deception, Casey did not fail quite as bad as he was led to believe.

As the agents began, one slammed his fist on the table, getting Casey's undivided attention. Agent Dukes, taking the lead in this interview, started. "Franklin, you indicated to us you were willing to talk about the Kirtland kidnappings, is that correct?"

"Yes, sir," replied Casey.

"First, before we begin, we don't think you were personally involved with the torture or murdering of the two boys, but we do believe you were involved in the kidnapping. If you are truthful with us, we will speak with the district attorney and try to get a deal for you. Does that sound fair to you?" said Agent Dukes.

Franklin Casey nodded his head in agreement.

Agent Dukes turned on the tape recorder.

"Alright, let's begin. My name is Agent Dukes of the FBI and I am interviewing Franklin Casey from Columbus, Ohio. Today is September 9, 1963, and the time is 7:30 pm," said Agent Dukes. Dukes continued, "Mr. Casey, do you willingly give us your statement and promise it will be truthful and accurate?"

"Yes, sir," replied Casey.

"How do you know Teddy Bowman?" began Dukes.

"We met years ago in a bar someplace. I don't even remember where the bar was, Euclid or Cleveland maybe," said Casey.

"Were you and Bowman in prison together? If so, for how long and for what crime?" said Dukes.

"We were convicted of kidnapping a boy. We were sentenced to ten years. We did eight years at the Ohio State Penitentiary," said Casey.

"When did you get out of prison?" asked Dukes.

"1960," replied Casey.

"What have you been doing for the past three years?" asked Dukes.

"Me and Bowman have been kicking back in Chesterland. He's working and I'm just between jobs," replied Casey. "Lately we've been thinking about making some fast money, know what I mean?"

"No, please tell me all about it," said Dukes.

"Kidnapping is easy money," said Casey. "You snatch someone, make a couple of calls, and get paid. The cops are stupid. Parents will do anything to get their kid back. They only caught us because we left someone alive. Shit, forget I said that!"

The agent inside the room tried his best not to smile, however, the witnesses outside the interrogation room all looked at each other with astonishment.

As stupid as Franklin Casey was, even he knew he just stepped in a big pile of crap.

Casey hung his head.

"Where were you the first week of June this past year?" asked Dukes.

"Ah, maybe Kirtland," said Casey.

"Maybe you were in Kirtland or you actually were in Kirtland?" asked Dukes.

"Yeah, we were in Kirtland," replied Casey.

"Who were you with?" asked Dukes.

"I was with Teddy Bowman," replied Casey.

What Franklin Casey failed to realize was, he was given some of the answers to these questions during the polygraph test. He knew about being in Kirtland in June, about the kidnapping of four boys, about the death of two of the boys, communicating with cardboard poster signs, in short almost everything he needed for this interview.

Agent Dukes stepped out of the room for a couple of minutes. The men outside the room were congratulating him and slapping him on the back as he went back into the room with a drink of water for Casey.

Agent Dukes decided to go in for the kill.

"Whose idea was it to kidnap the four Kirtland boys?" asked Dukes.

"It wasn't my idea. It was Bowman's idea. He wanted to make some easy money," said Casey.

"Why did you and your partner need to make money?" asked Dukes.

"Bowman wanted to move to Hollywood. He thinks he is handsome and maybe he could be in the movies," replied Casey.

"Did you and Bowman always wear black clothes, shoes and gloves when you saw the kidnapped boys?" asked Dukes.

"Yeah, we always wore black clothes," replied Casey.

"Did you both cover your faces?" asked Dukes.

"Yeah, I think so," said Casey.

"How did you cover your faces?" asked Dukes.

"We wore a mask," replied Casey.

"Why didn't you ask for money from the boy's parents?" asked Dukes.

"We were going to, but Bowman killed one of the boys, so we didn't know what to do," replied Casey.

"How did you communicate with the boys?" asked Dukes.

"We wrote stuff down on cardboard," replied Casey.

"Which boy did Bowman kill and how did he kill him?" asked Dukes.

"I don't know the names, I never asked. He killed one of them. I think he strangled him," said Casey. "After that, we couldn't ask for any money."

"What about the other boy? How did he die?" asked Dukes.

"I don't remember for sure. I think Bowman shot him a couple of times," replied Casey.

"What did you do with the bodies?" asked Dukes.

"We buried one of them in Chesterland. I am not sure where," said Casey.

"How about the other boy?" asked Dukes.

"I think we dropped him off at some park. We didn't have time to bury him," responded Casey.

Again, Casey was given this information during his polygraph test.

"Why didn't you or Bowman kill the other two boys?" asked Dukes.

"I didn't want them to die, so I suggested we take them somewhere and let them go," replied Casey. "Franklin was pissed off at me cause he wanted to kill them too, but he took them for a ride and let them go."

With that, Agent Dukes left the room. He told the others he needed to take a shower.

"Do you think we have enough to get a conviction?" asked Mr. Coletti.

Agent Wilhelm responded, "There are some inconsistencies, but, in my opinion, you should be able to convict Bowman, especially with Casey's testimony. Also, if you drive them back to Painesville, take two cars and keep these idiots apart."

District Attorney Coletti could not thank the FBI enough. "We appreciate your help in this case. We learned some great interrogation techniques," said Coletti.

"Your welcome," said Agent Wilhelm. "We plan to execute a warrant on the Bowman and Casey property in Chesterfield tomorrow. If you do not mind, the FBI forensic team is ready and well prepared to handle the search. You are welcome to join us. Either way, we'll let you know if we find anything."

The sheriff agreed to meet the FBI at the Chesterland house the following morning.

Based solely on Casey's confession, the sheriff and district attorney arrested both Teddy Bowman and Franklin Casey then drove them back to Painesville, Ohio.

Chapter 21

Bowman Trial

After returning to Painesville, Teddy Bowman and Franklin Casey were arraigned in the Lake County Courthouse on four counts kidnapping, four counts torture, and four counts unlawful imprisonment, plus one count of manslaughter in the death of Tony Sawyer.

The DA did not charge either defendant in the murder of Kenny Lang due to the police not being able to locate the body. Both defendants pled not guilty and were remanded to the Lake County Jail

The plea deal with Franklin Casey was straightforward. Casey agreed to testify against Teddy Bowman, pled guilty to four counts of kidnapping a minor and in return he received a twenty-five year to life sentence. The state did a masterful job on Casey, and he was more than ready to testify against his partner.

The trial of Teddy Bowman was a huge event, especially for the very small Lake County. By the end of 1963, the trial was set to begin and the jury was selected.

If it were up to the residents of Lake County, they would have skipped the trial and hung Teddy Bowman, right there and then. The entire events of the summer and fall in Lake County were a roller coaster ride for the citizens. Finding out that four boys were kidnapped, and two missing or dead, was too much for many of the citizens.

The defense attorney, Scott Pruitt, did his best to find a jury of Bowman's peers, however most of the all-Christian jurors had young children and were law-abiding citizens themselves. The jury would have a difficult time sympathizing with life-long felons.

The state began with their forensic experts from the FBI. These specialists would be hard to impeach, but the defense attorney did his best to do just that.

Both the defense and prosecution agreed that the first witness was an expert in the field of forensic science. During the search of the Bowman property, a small amount of rope was secured and several blank cardboard signs. The witness testified the rope was the same type as the rope that bound Jake Adams and Pete Peterson. He also testified the signs were like those described by the young boys.

The defense attorney cross-examined the witness hard. He asked if the ropes were identical to those found on the boys or only similar. Then he asked if any blood evidence, hair evidence, or fingerprints were found. The forensic expert answered that none of that evidence was found. In addition, since none of the cardboard signs were recovered, the judge threw out the sign evidence.

Mr. Coletti objected to throwing out the sign evidence, but the objection was overruled.

The next witness recalled seeing Bowman and Casey driving through Kirtland around the time of the kidnappings.

The next witness, also from the FBI, brought news clipping about the missing boys found inside the Bowman home. There were audible gasps from the audience, which the judge quickly admonished.

Mr. Scott asked the witness if it was possible for people other than the defendant to save newspaper clippings.

The witness answered, yes, it was possible.

The Lake County Coroner was the next witness. He testified that Tony Sawyer died from complications of asthma. Additionally, he testified Tony would most likely still be alive if he had been properly treated and had access to an inhaler. The defense attorney was unable to discredit or impeach the coroner.

The next witness was the emergency room doctor who testified Jake Adams and Pete Peterson both suffered from dehydration and were both malnourished. There was no cross-examination of this witness.

Then Jake Adams took the stand. Jake testified about sleeping out with his best friends, Pete, Kenny, and Tony, and that during the night, they were kidnapped at gunpoint. The kidnappers never said even one word. The boys wore hoods and were marched off the mountain and into a vehicle. Then the boys were driven to an undisclosed location where they were held in a cage.

The audience moaned, and the jurors wiped tears from their eyes.

Jake testified that Tony informed the kidnappers he had asthma and would need an additional inhaler. Jake testified about calling out for Tony, but he never answered them and about calling out for Kenny. Jake told about he and Pete deciding to try for an escape just before they were released. Jake told of the kidnappers forcing them to wear hoods then driving them somewhere far away and releasing them. Jake said both Pete and himself thought they would be killed and left somewhere. Jake told the jury about the kidnappers poking them with sharp objects, starving the boys, playing Russian roulette, and blasting them with water. Jake also told about the kidnappers playing loud music all night long. When asked if he ever saw the defendant, Jake replied he never saw either of the men, but they were physically about the same size as the kidnappers.

Overall, Jake did a wonderful job. The jury was obviously affected by his testimony.

The defense attorney chose to go easy on Jake. He asked again if he ever heard or saw the abductors. Jake said no he never saw them. Then Mr. Scott asked

Jake how he could be so sure the defendant kidnapped him. Jake said he could not be one hundred percent sure.

After Jake, Pete Peterson testified. Pete told the same story as Jake, the sleepout, the kidnapping, the torture, the absence of his friends, Tony's asthma and the release of Jake and him at the park.

Once again, Mr. Scott went easy on Pete. He did not want to lose the jury altogether. Mr. Scott did manage to get Pete to say once again, he never saw the kidnappers or heard their voices. Mr. Scott was doing a very good job, poking holes in the already weak defense.

As Pete left the witness stand, he could not help but notice a familiar face, Kimberly Roberts, who was in the courtroom just about every day. Pete nodded his head at Kimberly who smiled in return.

The next witness, Franklin Casey, was the prosecution's star witness. Casey described the entire set of events including the actual kidnapping, speaking with the boys using cardboard signs and the drive home to Chesterland. Regarding Tony's death, Casey said he thought Bowman smothered the boy.

Tony's mother, sitting in the court, busted out crying and was escorted out of the courthouse by friends.

Casey then said Bowman told him that he shot Kenny Lang, although he did not witness the actual crime. The entire courtroom was silent. You could hear a pin drop. Casey had testified almost exactly like his original statement to the FBI. The prosecutor was pleased with the job Casey did.

The defense attorney had to destroy Casey and his testimony. Scott was able to get Casey to admit he never actually saw the alleged murders. Since there was no forensic evidence, Mr. Scott did not need to go after that testimony. He would deal with the lack of forensic evidence in his closing statement.

Mr. Scott did confuse Casey several times. Casey could not remember how many cages there were altogether, who wrote out the signs, or who sprayed the boys with water. Casey did admit that he was receiving a life sentence for his testimony and that he was a prior felon. Mr. Coletti objected, but since Casey made himself look like a saint, the judge allowed it.

The closing arguments were straightforward. Mr. Scott spoke at length about the lack of evidence. There was no gun, no cages, no van, and he was never seen or heard during the alleged kidnapping. Scott spoke about Bowman trying to change his life. Bowman was working and trying to save money. Bowman wanted to move to a warmer climate. The defense attorney inadvertently gave the prosecution motive.

Mr. Coletti went after Bowman in his closing arguments. Since it was brought up that Bowman was changing his life and trying to save money, the prosecutor was able to tell the jury that Bowman was a prior felon and there was one place he could get the kind of money he needed to move, by kidnapping four young boys and holding them for ransom. Mr. Coletti told the jury that if Bowman had not killed Tony Sawyer, he would have asked for ransom money from the parents.

The jury was out for less than a day. They returned with a unanimous verdict, guilty on all counts.

Teddy Bowman was beside himself. The evidence was flimsy at best. Terry Bowman was guilty of many things, but not in this case. If not for the testimony of Franklin Casey, this never would have gone to trial. *Casey is a stupid idiot,* thought Bowman. He was hopeful they would send Casey to the same prison as him, and preferably in the same cell. He would make sure Casey did not last a week.

At sentencing, the defense argued that Teddy Bowman lived a difficult life and he was trying to work and be a better member of society. Scott tried to tell the jury that the entire case was circumstantial and nobody should be sentenced to life on such flimsy evidence.

In the end, this jury would have convicted Santa Claus. Somebody had to pay for such a heinous crime. Perhaps, if Bowman had been truthful and admitted where he buried the body of Kenny Lang and what really happened to Tony Sawyer, then maybe the jury would have sentenced him to life with a possibility of parole. However, Bowman was arrogant throughout the entire trial and showed obvious contempt for the jury and the proceedings. The kidnapping of four boys, four promising young boys, deserved no less than a life sentence at the Ohio Penitentiary.

The following morning, Bowman was formally sentenced to life in prison without the possibility of parole. The felony kidnapping of four minors and torture brought a life sentence all by itself. Plus, if the body of Kenny Lang was ever found, Bowman could be looking at a possible death sentence. The DA held the first-degree murder charge in his pocket to use on a later day.

Everyone seemed pleased with the verdicts. Mr. and Mrs. Lang held each other close while the Sawyer family would have preferred to just shoot Bowman and Casey. Nothing would bring back their son and they wanted Bowman to pay.

Jake did not have much to say about the verdict. However, he hoped the outcome might help him cope better and get on with his life. Pete Peterson smiled and laughed at Bowman. Pete, like his parents, hated Bowman and never wanted to see either man again.

Pete did notice that Kimberly Roberts seemed pleased with the verdict. Pete did not understand why Kimberly was happy. After all, Pete only met her the one time when she drove him home.

Chapter 22

~~~~~~~~~

The Verdict

On the way home from the courthouse, Kimberly stopped off at the Kirtland High School and picked up her sister. Sally opened the door of the van and could see her sister was in high spirits.

"Let's go home and open a bottle of wine," said Kimberly.

"What are you so happy about?" asked Sally.

"The verdict came in today for Teddy Bowman. He is going away for life without the possibility of parole!" exclaimed Kimberly.

Sally replied, "Why does that make you so happy? You know he didn't do it."

"I'll tell you why," said Kimberly. "There are two reasons. Even though he is innocent of this crime, he is a felon and previously kidnapped a boy. Then, he tried to collect ransom off the boy. Secondly, this means we are off the hook. Now we can go on with our lives."

"I'm not sure I can put this behind me," said Sally. "The jury convicted an innocent man. That makes me feel sick to my stomach."

"That's because you are so kind-hearted," replied Kimberly. "Please, try and forget this. I don't want to go to prison. Remember, these boys attacked our way of life, and their anger and selfishness killed Daddy."

"Yes, you are absolutely right. I will try to forget this whole thing ever happened. I'm glad we are safe," said Sally.

During dinner, Kimberly opened a bottle of wine for the occasion. Kimberly had a friend who often sold her alcohol. This was a special occasion if there ever was one.

"You know, Bowman will probably get out of prison someday, and they'll go on to live long lives," said Kimberly.

"I know that, but it doesn't make me feel better. Two men are going to prison for crimes they did not commit," replied Sally.

Sally was not sure what she should do but she knew that these men were innocent and something needed to be done.

Jake was starting to settle down a bit. He was finally able to sleep at night and was not afraid of his own shadow. Pete never seemed to have a problem coping. He took the news of the guilty verdict in stride. Pete knew that Jake was struggling and vowed to spend time with Jake to try to help him.

Now that the trial was over, both boys could return to school. At first, the boys were on call to testify so they chose to stay out of school. If nothing else, the boys had the chance to look Bowman and Casey in the eyes.

Bowman and Casey matched the physical appearance of the kidnappers. Bowman was taller and thinner while Casey was a little heavier. These physical descriptions were etched in the minds of both Jake and Pete. The boys could remember the taller man, holding the gun, standing watch over the boys, while the shorter man opened the cages to put the food inside.

Pete and Jake began to spend more time with each other after school.

"I really miss Tony and Kenny," said Jake. "I miss them every day. I often wonder what happened to Kenny."

"Try not to think about it so much," replied Pete. "I know that's impossible to do, but you'll drive yourself crazy thinking about it. I miss them too, all the time."

"Should we have tried to escape after they killed Tony?" said Jake. "I mean if we could have escaped, it is possible Kenny would still be alive."

"We'll never know. If they caught us trying to escape, they might have killed all of us. I think they could have killed us if they really wanted to," said Pete. "There is something else bothering me."

"What's that?" asked Jake.

"Why didn't these guys ever talk to us? Also, why did they need to hold a gun on us?" asked Pete. "We're just kids. These guys could have messed us up anytime they felt like it."

Jake responded, "So what are you trying to say?"

"I don't know. There are a few things that just don't add up," replied Pete. "There wasn't really any evidence. The partner, what is his name… Casey, seemed like a real nut job. How could a jury ever convict Bowman?"

"There is something else bothering you, what is it?" asked Jake.

Pete replied, "Well, Kimberly Roberts was at the trial almost every day. I went to the spring dance with her sister Sally. Why was she there? When the verdict was read, Kimberly seemed almost relieved, why is that? Tomorrow at school, I'm going to ask Sally why her sister was at the trial. I'll let you know what she says," said Pete.

"Alright, I gotta go now. I have a shit load of homework. I'll talk to you tomorrow," said Jake.

The next morning, when Sally and Pete were in homeroom, Pete decided to have a little chat with Sally.

"Hi Sally, so what did you do over the summer?" asked Pete.

"Not much," replied Sally. "I just stayed around the house with Kimberly. Sorry to hear about your friends. I heard that the trial is over and the jury convicted that man."

"Yeah, they convicted him," said Pete. "But, I'm really not so sure he is guilty. I mean, how do I really know? I never saw their faces, and they never spoke to us."

"Looks like homeroom is going to start pretty soon. We better get to our seats," said Sally.

"Maybe we can talk later, like after school," said Pete.

"No, I can't stay after school. My sister wanted me to do some chores around the farm," replied Sally.

"What farm?" asked Pete.

"Our family owns a fruit and vegetable farm over on Route 6," replied Sally.

Pete's stomach dropped to the floor. He wondered if the Roberts' farm was the same farm he and his friends stole from, almost daily. Pete knew this farm very well. He was quickly reminded of the time he and the other boys destroyed some apples and watermelons on a farm on Route 6. Pete hoped this was not the same farm.

Pete excused himself and took his seat. After school, Pete sought out his long-time friend.

"Jake, I need to talk to you. Can you come over to my house after school? Nobody will be home and we can speak in private," said Pete.

"Sure," replied Jake. "Are you alright?"

"I'm not really sure. Let's talk later," replied Pete.

"Alright, see you soon," responded Jake.

Jake walked home from the bus stop to drop his books off and grab a snack. Jake told his mom he was walking to Pete's house. Mrs. Adams was happy to see Jake finally going outside by himself.

Pete was waiting for Jake in his front yard. Jake and Pete walked around to the back of the house and sat down on a lawn chair.

"So, what's up," asked Jake.

"Let me ask you a question," replied Pete. "Is it possible, the men who abducted us were not men at all, but women?"

Jake started to laugh aloud. "What the hell are you talking about?" said Jake. "Are you crazy or just messing around? How could women kidnap and torture us?"

"Will you just listen to me for a minute?" replied Pete. "I'm serious. It's just a question. Do you think it is possible women took us?"

"No, I don't think the kidnappers were women," said Jake. "So, why do you think they might be women?"

"Well, let me walk you through this," said Pete. "First of all, we never saw the faces of the kidnappers or heard their voices. They held up signs for us to read. Why didn't they speak? They could have disguised their voices."

"Okay," Jake said shrugging. "I'm with you so far."

"Secondly, they never put their hands on us or even touched us. Wouldn't violent men push us around?" said Pete.

"Do you think they convicted the wrong guys? How could they? One of them confessed," replied Jake.

"Okay, just listen. They never touched us or spoke to us. Do you remember me telling you about the girl I went to the dance with?" asked Pete.

"Yeah, I remember," responded Jake.

"Her name is Sally Roberts. Her family owns a fruit and vegetable farm. Do you know where it is? I'll tell you, it's over on Route 6," said Pete. "You know what else? After the dance, her sister picked us up in a van and they drove me home."

"Also," continued Pete, "Sally's sister was in court, almost every day. She seemed overjoyed when that Bowman guy was convicted. I only met her that one time. Her name is Kimberly. Why would she care so much about the verdict?"

"What does she look like?" asked Jake.

"Kimberly is a couple of inches taller than Sally," replied Pete. "She told me she was 18 or 19 years old. She is very pretty."

"Is it the same farm, the one we raided many times?" asked Jake.

"I don't know," replied Pete. "But that could be a very important question. Let me continue. I found out today, their father died from a heart attack, just about the same time we cut up all those apples. The police never found out why these men even kidnapped us. Our parents are not rich and they never asked for money. So, what did they want?"

"That's also been bugging me since they let us go," replied Jake.

"Also, why did they let us go? They drove us all over the place so we couldn't figure out where we were being held," said Pete. "We could have been a half a mile from home this whole time."

"Why would someone kidnap and torture us for cutting up a few apples?" said Jake.

"It wasn't just a few apples," replied Pete. "We cut the shit out of as many apples we could reach then kicked in dozens of watermelons. We did that because the farmer chased you. We wanted him to know he pissed us off."

"Pete, what are you saying?" asked Jake.

"I think it's possible that the kidnappers were not men at all," said Pete. "I think the two sisters kidnapped us. Kimberly was the taller one and Sally the shorter one."

"Oh my God," said Jake. "How do we find out for sure? Do we tell anyone? We'll be a laughingstock in town. Getting abducted and beat up by two girls."

"We have to be sure. I tried talking to Sally at school about her summer vacation," replied Pete. "She didn't want to talk. She seemed very nervous. I will try talking to her tomorrow. I need to know exactly where their farm is."

"Okay, let's talk tomorrow after school. There is a lot to think about," said Jake.

Jake walked back home and sat down to do his homework. Mrs. Adams asked Jake if he was feeling all right because he looked a little pale. Jake assured her he was all right, just a little tired.

After dinner, Jake did his homework then went to bed early. Jake was tossing and turning. He was having difficulty falling asleep. Jake kept going over his discussion with Pete from earlier that day.

Eventually Jake fell asleep. However, something startled him and he abruptly woke up. Jake was having trouble focusing, so he cleared the grit from his eyes. As Jake looked up, he could see two men staring down at him. They were wearing all black clothes and carrying a gun.

Jake screamed.

His mother and father came flying into Jake's room and woke him up from his nightmare.

Jake wondered if he was ever going to feel safe again, especially since Pete almost convinced him the real kidnappers might still be out there.

Chapter 23

Curiosity

Before school, Sally decided to speak to Kimberly. Sally was nervous about the conversation she had the previous day with Pete.

"Kimberly, I need to talk to you," said Sally.

"That doesn't sound good," replied Kimberly. "You go right ahead. Do you need some money?"

"I wish that was all I needed to speak with you about. I'm afraid I may have screwed up yesterday," replied Sally.

Sally continued, "Here goes. Yesterday Pete came up to me before homeroom. He was asking questions about the location of the farm. I told him the farm was on Route 6. He said he was not sure the convicted men were even guilty. He wanted to ask more questions, but I excused myself."

Kimberly responded, "That doesn't sound too bad. You can't keep excusing yourself or he may become more curious as to why you leave every time the subject comes up."

"I'm afraid I do not think as quickly as you do," said Sally.

"Try and find out what is on Pete's mind today. We may need to make a serious decision," said Kimberly.

"We can't kill anyone else. The jury already convicted Bowman," replied Sally.

"I know. Maybe we can do something else, I am not sure. See what Pete has to say. If he gets too curious, invite him and Jake over," said Kimberly. "If they believe we are guilty, there is no way they will come over."

"Alright, I hope I can do this," replied Sally.

Kimberly dropped Sally off at school and wished her good luck.

Before homeroom, Sally decided to find Pete. This way, Pete would see she was not hiding from him.

"Hi Pete," said Sally. "What is going on? It seemed like you had more on your mind yesterday."

Pete was taken by surprise. Maybe he was wrong about Sally and Kimberly.

Pete replied, "I was only curious why Kimberly was in the courthouse almost every day."

"Kimberly is bored. We have farmhands to help with our orchard and vegetables. Kimberly thought you were nice and she liked you very much. She only wanted the jury to convict Bowman. That is the only reason," replied Sally nonchalantly.

Pete was confused. He did not expect this answer. He really didn't know what to expect.

Sally continued, "Since we are back in school and your life is back on track, maybe you would like to come over? We could hang out. If you like, bring Jake with you."

"Yes, maybe we will," said Pete. "I'll get back to you on that one."

Pete was unclear what just happened. It seemed obvious he was wrong about Kimberly and Sally.

Later that afternoon, Pete shared his findings with Jake. The information pleased Jake since he knew the men who kidnapped them were no longer a threat. Pete was also happy. He still wanted to date Sally if she would go out with him. If nothing else, Pete would accept Sally's invitation to hang out. He was looking forward to it.

The following morning, Sally asked Pete if he would like to come over after school. Smiling, Sally asked if he knew where she lived. Pete assured Sally he was sure he knew her location.

Pete and Jake arrived at the Roberts' ranch around 4:30 pm that afternoon.

Jake appeared nervous as he spoke with Pete.

"I've never seen the front of the farmhouse. I've walked past here a thousand times and never paid any attention to it," said Jake.

"I hear you," replied Pete. "I hope this is not a big mistake."

"What do you mean," replied Jake.

"Well, Sally is nice, but her sister is a little different. Whenever I get a car, I'd like to take Sally out," said Pete.

Pete and Jake approached the front door. Everything was quiet. Pete knocked on the door a couple of times. Eventually, the boys heard Sally's voice saying, "Come in and have a seat," said Sally. "We will be with you in a minute."

Walking into the living room, Kimberly said to the boys, "Hi boys, how are you both doing?"

Jake and Pete both told Kimberly they were doing all right.

Pete said to Kimberly, "I was a little surprised you were in court so often. Why were you there, if you don't mind me asking?"

"Well," said Kimberly, "You are a friend of Sally's so I was curious what happened to you. I was there to support you and your friend. I wanted to see for myself that Bowman was convicted and got punished."

"Thanks," said Pete. "It was nice to see a friendly face. I was afraid to face Bowman alone so sometimes I just looked towards you."

"That's kind of you to say," said Kimberly. "I'll leave you guys alone. Have fun!"

Sally took Jake and Pete on a tour around the farm. She showed the boys their farm equipment and the orchards.

Pointing towards the boarded-up house, Pete asked, "Who lives in that house?"

Sally told them their grandparents lived there until they died several years earlier.

Walking through the orchard, Sally said, "I'm sure you both know all about apple trees, right?"

Neither Pete nor Jake knew what Sally was referring to, but both boys had an uneasy feeling. Jake was starting to believe the Roberts' girls knew more about their ordeal than they were saying.

Jake and Pete excused themselves and left through the woods. Pete also caught the negative comment from Sally.

"I still think we should talk to our parents," said Pete.

"Okay," replied Jake. "Let's sit down with our parents tonight. I'll ask my mom and dad to drive over to your house. You should probably tell your parents to expect us after dinner."

Later that evening, Mr. and Mrs. Adams drove Jake over to the Peterson home. While sitting down in the living room, Pete began the discussion.

"Folks," said Pete. "We have something to say and we're sure you will think we are both crazy, but we have to say it anyways. We are not sure anymore that Casey and Bowman were the kidnappers."

"What do you mean?" said Mr. Peterson.

"Please just listen to us before saying anything," said Jake. "You probably don't know this, but we did a lot of bad things before we were kidnapped. We ruined some property, had a guy's car towed and destroyed some fruit at a local orchard."

"You did not!" exclaimed Mrs. Adams.

"Yes, we did," said Pete. "We've been thinking a lot lately and wanted to share some things with all of you. We don't believe Bowman and Casey had a reason to take us. They never asked for money and they released Jake and me, both unharmed."

"Don't forget that Casey confessed," said Mrs. Peterson.

"We know that, but please listen," said Pete.

"The Roberts farm is over on Route 6. It's just a short walk through the woods. Nearly every time we slept out, we would stop there first to swipe some fruit," said Jake.

Pete began, "We would usually take some watermelon, grapes and sometimes a couple of apples. Most of the time the old farmer would chase us off his land. Sometimes he chased us with his car. One time he almost caught Jake."

"Yes, if not for Pete and the other boys holding open the barbed wire for me, the farmer probably would have caught me," said Jake.

Pete continued, "Anyways, after the last time this guy chased us, we went to his farm and destroyed dozens of apples and watermelons. Shortly afterward, the old farmer had a heart attack and died."

"It's possible his daughters hate us because their dad died," said Jake. "What if we were captured by girls, dressed like men?"

"Are you saying the daughters have a motive to hurt all you boys?" asked Mr. Peterson.

"It's possible," replied Pete. "The younger daughter goes to school with me. I went to the spring dance with her. After the dance, her older sister picked us up and drove me home. She had a van, just like the kidnappers."

"We were just at the farm," said Jake. "At first Sally seemed nice, but then she started talking about the apple trees and how Pete and I should know all about apple trees. The discussion became very strange."

"The kidnappers never spoke to us. Why didn't they speak to us? The kidnappers never manhandled us. Why didn't they throw us around? They never showed their faces. These people did a remarkable job hiding their identities," said Pete. "We just are concerned the wrong people are going to prison. Maybe we should speak to the district attorney?"

"I don't think young girls could do this," said Mr. Adams.

"What part of this do you think girls are not capable of?" said Mrs. Adams. "I'll have you know girls are just as vindictive as men. Maybe even more so."

"Alright, I'll call Mr. Coletti and ask for a sit down with all of us," said Mr. Adams. "We need to be sure."

Chapter 24

Sharing Suspicions

Mr. Adams was able to schedule an appointment with Mr. Coletti for the following Monday afternoon. Mr. and Mrs. Peterson picked up the boys from school and met Mr. and Mrs. Adams at the DA's office. Mr. Coletti invited the Lake County sheriff to the meeting.

Pete began the discussion. "For many reasons we will discuss, we are not convinced the right men are in prison. Matter of fact, we are not sure the kidnappers are men."

"Go ahead boys, I'm all ears," said Mr. Coletti.

Pete and Jake laid out their concerns. Pete discussed going with Sally Roberts to the dance and her sister bringing them home. He told everyone Kimberly seemed interested to know where he and his friends lived and she owned a van. Pete also told everyone about Kimberly being a frequent court visitor. Then Pete spoke about Sally and the remarks she made to both boys at the farm. Sally told Pete and Jake they should be familiar with where the apple trees are. Pete took this to mean that Sally knew Pete and Jake were previous visitors to the farm. The conversation was very strange, and when the discussion was over, the boys abruptly went home.

Jake also had some concerns. The kidnappers never spoke to them, never touched them, and kept the boys in line with a gun. That seemed very odd to Jake. Looking back, especially when Kenny was yelling at the kidnappers, why didn't they come into his cage and throw him around? Instead, they sprayed all the boys down with a water hose. These two appeared much bigger than either of the boys, yet they seemed unwilling to mix it up.

Pete told about the raid on the farm when all four boys stole fruit from the Roberts' farm and how, after the farmer chased them, they went back and destroyed apples and watermelons. Pete said all four boys did lots of bad things, stuff they were not proud of. Pete and Jake wondered if they gave someone a motive to hurt them.

The boys also heard the farmer died from a heart attack. The timing seemed to indicate he died shortly after chasing them. The boys wondered if Sally and Kimberly blamed them for their father's death and wanted to get even. The men Mr. Coletti convicted did not have a motive. If the motive was money, they could have made ransom calls before Tony died.

Mr. Coletti looked at the sheriff. Both men turned back to the boys and Mr. Coletti said, "We've considered many things over the past month or so. You are right. There has never been a clear motive. We were never sure Bowman would be convicted. We never presented real forensic evidence such as hair, blood or fingerprints. We found no such thing at the Bowman home or in either of their vehicles. That being said," continued Mr. Coletti, "We do have a confession. This alone is hard to dispute. We haven't charged anyone with Kenny Lang's disappearance or murder. We still have this charge we keep in the back pocket."

"The real question is, do we think women are capable of such a crime? Yes, we do. We don't have any concrete proof right now. The sheriff and I will visit the Roberts' farm to speak with both girls. We will call this a follow-up meeting. Also, we will not tell them about this meeting so please keep this to yourselves. If we can come up with a compelling reason, we will obtain a search warrant for their land and property. If we get a search warrant, we will bring the girls in for an informal chat while the search is conducted. Does that sound alright with you boys?"

"Yes, sir," replied both Jake and Pete.

On the way home, Mr. Adams told Jake he was sorry he didn't believe the boys sooner, but he was coming around to their way of thinking. Jake asked about stopping for dinner at the Dog N Suds, but Mr. Adams could see bad weather was fast approaching and thought they should get home.

Mr. Coletti and Sheriff Schultz decided to visit the Roberts' farm driving in a marked police car. They pulled into the driveway early in the morning, hoping to catch Kimberly. When the sheriff rang the doorbell, Kimberly promptly answered the door.

The first thing Mr. Coletti noticed was Kimberly's calm demeanor. She seemed to almost expect the visit. Mr. Coletti began asking some questions such as when did your father die, do you own the farm, do you and Sally work the property or do you have farm helpers, etc. Kimberly was gracious with her responses. She finally asked what the purpose was for the visit. The sheriff said they were visiting people around the immediate area because they were still looking for one of the boys.

Kimberly did not seem at all nervous with the questions. Either she was cool under pressure, she took no part in the kidnappings, or she was a psychopath.

Mr. Coletti and the sheriff left the farm feeling confident neither Kimberly nor her sister took any part in the kidnappings or murders. Coletti also felt all the law enforcement, including the DA's office, the Sheriff's Department and the FBI did their due diligence and should feel good about sending Casey and Bowman to jail. Also, there wasn't probable cause for a search warrant. Plus, the case concerning three of the boys was considered closed. Further investigations would have to wait until Kenny Lang's body was found. Mr. Coletti offered to sit down with the boys and their parents to help give everyone some closure.

Soon after the visit ended, Kimberly drove off and stopped at the high school to take Sally out of class. When Sally saw her sister, she was surprised.

"Is everything alright?" asked Sally.

"Sure is, I just need your help. Can you leave school?" asked Kimberly.

"I think so. I have all my homework assignments. I'd just be missing physical education and study hall. No big thing," replied Sally.

Kimberly responded, "Alright, let's go. Now please!"

Sally was sure something was wrong. When they drove out of the parking lot, Sally asked Kimberly what the problem was.

"The cops came to see me today," said Kimberly.

"What! Oh my God. What did they want?" asked Sally.

"They were nosing around. I think your friend said something to them. I knew we should have killed all four of them," said Kimberly. "You and I need to work on your story because sooner or later, they will want to speak to you."

"Why would they suspect anything?" asked Sally.

"Like I said, I think Pete and Jake said something. You should keep your comments about the boys knowing where our fruit trees are to yourself," replied Kimberly.

"I promise, I will from now on," said Sally.

"If you speak with Pete again, just keep your cool. If he asks you out, you would be better off saying no. That should keep him from asking more questions," said Kimberly.

Later that evening, gale force winds ripped through Lake County. Everyone was encouraged to stay indoors and small boats were prohibited on the lake.

About five miles off the Mentor Headlands shoreline, high winds and violent waves forced a human hand and a bloated body to the surface. The following morning, pleasure boaters came across the disturbing scene and called the police. Due to exposure from inside the lake, the body was in extremely poor condition, however it seemed to be the body of a young male, between 13 to 19 years old.

The body was sent to the Lake County coroner. However, it would prove difficult to identify. This boy appeared to have been shot three times. The coroner had his suspicions, but the process could take days if not weeks. If this was the Lang boy, the coroner hoped Mr. Bowman would get the death penalty.

Chapter 25

Capital Crimes

Frank Coletti, the Lake County district attorney, paced back and forth waiting for the news. Earlier that morning he asked Rick Schultz, the Lake County sheriff, to send a deputy to Chesterland, Ohio to acquire the dental records of Kenny Lang, the sixteen-year-old boy who was kidnapped earlier that year. Coletti looked at his watch. He knew by now the dental records were delivered and were going through the process of identification. Coletti also knew in his heart the dental records were those of Kenny Lang.

Earlier that week, the body of a male was discovered and retrieved from Lake Erie, only a few miles from Mentor on the Lake. Coletti thought it would be statistically impossible for the body to belong to anyone other than Kenny Lang, but protocol dictated the body go through a rigorous autopsy. First to determine the name of the decedent and secondly to determine the cause of death.

Late that afternoon, Coletti was notified the coroner and sheriff were on their way to his office. Coletti sat at his conference table, patiently waiting for their arrival.

The coroner began, "The male body has been positively identified as the remains of Kenny Lang, sixteen-year-old male from Kirtland, Ohio. Although in very poor condition, dental records positively identify the body. Additionally, we have determined Kenny Lang was shot three times, once in the arm, once in the shoulder and the fatal shot in the forehead. Bullets we retrieved have been sent to ballistics to determine the caliber of the bullet and type of weapon used in the shooting. We are very confident the bullets came from a 22 Caliber handgun, but ballistics will positively tell us the origin. We also determined, since there was no fluid present in the boy's lungs, he was dead before going into the lake. The death is ruled a homicide."

Frank Coletti laid his head down on the table. After a short time, Coletti slowly lifted his head and began to speak. "Thank you all very much for your diligent service and quick results. Regarding the identity of the body, I think we felt all along how this kidnapping would end. Please keep this quiet for the time being. I don't want any of this information to leave the room. Rick, please drive to the Lang's home and bring them both to the medical examiner's office. As a formality, they need to identify the body. Also, please notify Agent Wilhelm at the FBI. They worked very hard on this case and deserve to be notified. I will be preparing charges against Terry Bowman and Franklin Casey for the first-degree murder of Kenny Lang. I pray they both are sentenced to death then go straight to hell."

Later that day, Mr. and Mrs. Lang arrived at the medical examiner's office. Although they tried to prepare themselves, they had no idea how badly their son was decomposed. Reluctantly, both Mr. and Mrs. Lang informed both the coroner and deputy the body behind the glass was in fact their son. The parents held each other and cried.

Later that afternoon Frank Coletti met with his team of prosecutors to discuss filing charges against Bowman and Casey for the Lang boy's murder. This meeting became quickly heated. More than half of the staff felt there was insufficient evidence to move forward against Bowman and Casey.

Dennis Anderson, the newest member of the team and lead prosecutor, began to lay out the pending case.

"First, this is a very perplexing case," said Anderson. "I've read all the court transcripts and all the evidence from the Bowman and Casey kidnapping trials. I have to say, I don't have any idea how Bowman and Casey were ever convicted. You had nearly zero physical evidence. You did, however, have the testimony of the two surviving boys, but they never heard the kidnappers speak nor could they identify their faces because the kidnappers wore masks the entire time. So, what did you have? You only had the testimony of Casey, a nitwit afraid of his own shadow. You also had a very emotional jury. A jury who wanted to convict someone just to bring some relief to the families of the boys and a community in shock from these heinous crimes. In my opinion, if Bowman and Casey win an appeal, the state will probably lose and these two will go free."

Frank Coletti slammed his fist down on the table. "Thanks for your opinion but we did convict Bowman and Casey!" exclaimed Coletti. "Your job is to discuss the pending murder trial against Bowman and Casey, not talk about a trial which you were no part of. Are you working for the state or for the defense?"

Anderson stood and looked directly at Coletti. "My job is to convict criminals," said Anderson. "I'm not an emotional guy, I look at the evidence and only the evidence. I'm telling you what you don't want to hear. I get that, but there is no evidence. Do you want to find the truth, or just get the conviction?"

"Sorry," said Coletti. "After hearing from the coroner and watching the family identify their son's body, it's hard not to get emotional. Alright, you are the voice of reason. So, what exactly are you saying to us?"

"I'm saying we need more time before charging Bowman and Casey," said Anderson. "We need to present a case, not only to win a conviction, but to also put everyone's minds at ease that we convicted the right people. I don't need to remind anyone a conviction of murder brings a possible death sentence."

Coletti began to speak but Anderson cut him off mid-sentence.

"Allow me to discuss the pending murder charges against Bowman and Casey," said Anderson. "Just hear me out."

"Alright," replied Coletti, "You have the floor."

Anderson began, "In my opinion we only have the identification of the body and cause of death. The coroner found three gunshot wounds. The fatal wound was to the head. We have no gun, no fingerprints, no blood evidence, no murder scene, and no witnesses. This lack of evidence is a recipe for a not-guilty verdict. We need time to collect more evidence. We need the police to canvas all around Kirtland to dig up potential witnesses. Without more evidence or a witness miraculously coming forward, we need another jail-house confession."

"What do you mean jail-house confession?" asked Coletti.

"First, we need to visit Bowman and Casey in prison to see about getting a confession," said Anderson.

"Tomorrow I will drive to the Ohio Penitentiary in Columbus to speak with Bowman and Casey and their associates. Let's start there, and then meet up the following morning. Mr. Coletti, can you ask the FBI if they can send an interrogator to the prison with me?"

"Certainly," said Coletti. "I'll try to get Agent Wilhelm, the original interrogator, to come with you. He made a connection with Casey before the first trial which helped facilitate the confession to the kidnapping. Also, I'm sorry for the outburst. I'm just a little emotional. Guilty as charged!"

Everyone in the room chuckled. Coletti's comments helped relieve some of the tension in the room.

Chapter 26

Penitentiary

Dennis Anderson and Agent Wilhelm arrived at the prison around noon. Wilhelm suggested they each interview either Casey or Bowman in separate interrogation rooms. Both men had a list of questions they wanted to ask each convict.

Anderson did not expect to have any luck with Bowman, and he was correct in his thinking. Bowman shut him down almost immediately.

Anderson began speaking, "Mr. Bowman, you should know we are looking into the murder of Kenny Lang, a young Kirtland boy found partially submerged in Lake Erie. Are you willing to talk with me about this matter?" asked Anderson.

Bowman stood and stared hatefully at Anderson. "Why don't you go and screw yourself," said Bowman.

Anderson replied, "No need to get personal. I merely asked you a question, a simple question I might add. If you didn't have anything to do with this crime, you really have nothing to worry about."

"That's what they said about the kidnapping charges," said Bowman, "and look at me now. I'm in prison, rotting away for a crime I did not commit."

"Whose fault is that?" said Anderson. "You refused to talk with the FBI or the sheriff about the crimes and you let Casey do all the talking. Like they say, whoever spills their guts gets the sweeter deal."

Anderson could feel he was getting to Bowman and he was enjoying himself a little too much. Anderson could barely keep himself from smiling.

Bowman could see the smirk on Anderson's face. "Glad you think this is funny," said Bowman. "Like I told you earlier, I have nothing to say and you sir. Go and screw yourself."

Anderson stood up, thanked Bowman for his time and excused himself from the room.

Agent Wilhelm was having a better time than Anderson did. Wilhelm met Casey in the interrogation room. Casey stood, shook the agent's hand and they both exchanged pleasantries.

Agent Wilhelm began, "Franklin, have you heard about the police finding the body of Kenny Lang in Lake Erie this past week?"

Casey's face turned white and he could only manage to shake his head.

Wilhelm was an experienced investigator. He knew to hold a few things back from the investigation before ever speaking to Casey.

"Let me be direct," said Wilhelm. "Did you have anything to do with the murder of Kenny Lang?"

"No way Jose," said Casey. "You can't pin this on me."

Agent Wilhelm continued, "Well let me ask you this. Since you confessed to kidnapping the four Kirtland boys, and Kenny Lang was one of those boys, how would you explain in court you didn't murder him?"

"I didn't kill anyone. Maybe Bowman killed him," said Casey. "I don't know. I'm trying for an appeal and my attorney told me to shut my mouth so that's what I'm gonna do. Sorry agent, but I'm not saying another word without a lawyer present."

Franklin Casey learned a few things since he came to prison, including how to shut up, Agent Wilhelm thought to himself.

Wilhelm and Anderson spent the rest of the afternoon interrogating other convicts housed near Bowman or Casey. A few of the men came up with some crazy stuff looking to make a deal, but none of the men knew a damn thing. Wilhelm and Anderson began the two-hour drive back to Painesville stopping for dinner along the way.

The following morning, Mr. Coletti and his staff met to discuss the pending murder charges against Bowman and Casey. Anderson asked Agent Wilhelm to join them due to his valuable perspective.

"Dennis, did you and Agent Wilhelm have the opportunity to interrogate Bowman and Casey?" asked Coletti.

"Yes sir, we sure did," replied Anderson. "I don't think you are going to want to hear what we have to say, but here goes."

Anderson continued, "Bowman shut down the interview almost immediately. He cussed at us a few times but refused to speak about the case. Casey was a little nicer but he took his attorney's advice and refused to speak to us as well. Bowman and Casey's new attorneys are getting organized to file an appeal," said Anderson. "From what I gather, they are appealing on the grounds of incompetent council and lack of physical evidence. After reading the transcripts, I think they have a point. Their attorneys never objected to much of anything. It seems to me they put very little effort in the case."

"Agent Wilhelm, do you have anything to add?" asked Mr. Coletti.

"No sir," replied Wilhelm. "We are not going to trick either man into a confession. To be totally honest with you, I don't think there is enough evidence to convict either man for murder. In my opinion, you should continue gathering evidence and continue interviewing the townspeople until you find something you can use. There is no statute of limitations for murder, so if you take a year or two before filing charges, so be it."

Assistant District Attorney Coletti stood and shook his head. It seemed he was almost in tears. "Alright," said Coletti. "We will do it your way. Let's kick the bushes and try to find some evidence."

Agent Wilhelm raised his hand to speak.

"Go right ahead," said Coletti.

"I think you and your office should go over the trial transcripts and prepare for the upcoming appeal," said Wilhelm. "If Bowman and Casey win an appeal, they stand a very good chance of either receiving a new trial or having the charges thrown out. Bowman and Casey could walk."

"I understand that," said Mr. Coletti. "We will hold off on filing murder charges and we will review the entire case to make sure we keep these two men in prison, where I believe they belong."

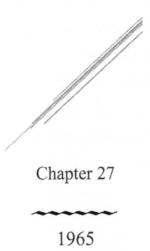

Chapter 27

~~~~~~~~

1965

Sally Roberts, now eighteen years old, excused herself early from her freshman English 101 class at the Ohio State University. Normally Sally was an exceptional student, however, she was struggling in her first semester.

As far away as Columbus, the newspapers were still reporting on the kidnapping and torture of four Kirtland teenagers and the two men, Bowman and Casey, winning the appeal and having all the charges dropped. Both men were free. Sally was worried the police might be looking at her and Kimberly. Sally was a wreck. No matter where she went and what she did she could not escape the news nor could she forget the horrible acts she and her sister committed only two years earlier. It was eating her up inside.

Sally felt pressured to attend the Ohio State University. First by the memory of her dead father and secondly by her sister. Sally promised her father one day she would attend his favorite college.

Sally initially wanted to attend Lakeland Community College in Kirtland, then maybe go on to a four-year college to finish her degree. However, after Jack's death, Kimberly decided since she was the oldest, she would stay home and operate the family farm while Sally went off to college. There was lots of help around the farm. The seasonal helpers harvested the apples, and other fruit while two permanent employees handled the day to day operations and harvested the vegetables. These men also kept a close eye on the main house. They thought of Kimberly and Sally as their daughters and were very protective. Kimberly took over the role of business manager, and she was very good at it. Ultimately, Kimberly wanted Sally to get a bachelor's degree in agriculture. Kimberly thought these were skills that could be useful on their fruit and vegetable farm.

Sally went back to her dorm and telephoned her sister. After the fourth ring, Kimberly picked up the phone.

"Hi baby," said Kimberly. "I was just thinking about you."

"Kimmy, I really need to talk to you. I'm having issues at school and I think we need some sister-to-sister face time right now," said Sally.

Sensing the stress in Sally's voice, Kimberly replied. "I can be in Columbus in two hours. Is this what you want?" asked Kimberly.

Sally responded, "Actually, I'd prefer to just come home for good, but right now I'd settle for a visit."

"Alright," said Kimberly. "How about we meet at noon at the store. Do you remember the store I'm referring to?" asked Kimberly.

This was one of the four hardware stores visited by the sisters when they went shopping for cages.

"I can hardly ever forget that store," said Sally. "See you there, bye!"

Shortly before noon, Kimberly pulled into the parking lot of the Buckeye Hardware Store. Sally was already waiting. Kimberly could immediately tell something was seriously wrong. Sally's eyes were red and she was crying.

"What's wrong honey?" asked Kimberly.

Sally replied, "You know what's wrong. I can't sleep. I can't eat and I sure as hell can't study," Sally continued, "I have to leave school and come home. I think I need to talk with somebody. Will you help me?"

"Talk to who?" Kimberly spat. "How about the police or the FBI? Would you like to speak with them for a friendly chat?"

"I knew you wouldn't understand," said Sally.

"No, I get it, but right now you are scaring the hell out of me," said Kimberly. "You do understand we can both go to prison for life if we are ever suspected of killing that boy, don't you?" asked Kimberly.

"I thought you told me that you would take the entire blame if we were ever caught," asked Sally.

"So, let me get this straight. You want me to go to prison for the rest of my life? Just so your conscience is clear. Is that what you are saying?" asked Kimberly.

"Hell no, I'm not saying that at all. I can't stay at school and I have nobody to talk to. If I drop out and come home, at least you and I can talk about things," replied Sally. "I would never turn you in. You are my blood, my only living relative. I would kill myself before that would ever happen."

"Alright," said Kimberly. "Let's go to the university and I'll help you leave school and take you home. Would that make you happy?"

Kimberly could sense Sally's stress level immediately lessening. Sally broke out in a big smile.

"I may decide to take some classes at Lakeland Community College," said Sally. "But for now, I just want to relax and try to cope with what we did."

Kimberly nodded her head in agreement.

Later that afternoon, Sally officially withdrew from school then followed Kimberly back to Kirtland, and to the security of their farm.

When the girls pulled into their driveway Sally could see the farm workers performing their daily chores. Sally missed the farm more than she ever thought possible. Everything still looked the same as before, although now, there was a calming presence. Before unpacking, Sally jumped on a tractor and went for a drive. She was all smiles.

Kimberly ran alongside the tractor, motioned for Sally to stop, and climbed up on the tractor to join her sister. The girls drove all around the farm until just after dark then went out for dinner to the Dog & Suds restaurant for a hot dog and some ice-cold root beer.

Sally woke the following morning to the sounds and smell of sizzling bacon. She jumped out of bed and nearly flew down the stairs. At the dinner table, Kimberly had laid out an awesome breakfast consisting of bacon, eggs, hash browns, and toast with homemade strawberry jelly. Sally quickly ate her breakfast then helped Kimberly clean up. Afterwards, Kimberly motioned for Sally to follow her outside to talk.

Kimberly began speaking, "I can't tell you how wonderful it is having you at home. I've been lonely myself and constantly worried about things, all sorts of things. Ever since Bowman and Casey were released, I've been on pins and needles. The police have been stopping at houses all over Kirtland, asking questions. They are searching for answers."

Kimberly continued, "We really need to make it a practice of only talking to each other while we are sitting outside or in the truck. You just never know who may be listening in. Secondly, yesterday you said something like you would kill yourself before ever turning me in. You don't actually have those thoughts, do you?"

Sally replied, "I've been in a very dark place. I can't forgive myself for the role I played in the kidnapping of those boys. It doesn't matter who pulled the trigger. I think in the eyes of God and the law we are both guilty. To answer your question, no, I want to live and I do not have suicidal thoughts."

Kimberly smiled and put her arms around her little sister to pull her in and give her a great big hug.

Chapter 28

Pete's Plan

Jake heard the doorbell ring and got up from the couch to answer it. When he opened the door, Jake was surprised to see Pete standing there. The two boys lost contact with each other since the trial of Teddy Bowman and Franklin Casey.

"Oh my God, how have you been?" asked Pete.

Jake opened the locked screen door and invited Pete into his house. Jake was still living with his parents in their home on Locust Drive.

Jake replied, "I'm okay, I guess. Good days and bad days."

"I thought you might still be struggling. I could tell the last time we spoke you were dealing with some issues," said Pete.

"Yeah, I have a few problems. I'm seeing a guy in Painesville. He's someone I can talk to. Seems to be helping a little," replied Jake.

"I'm glad you are getting help," said Pete. "I've all but forgotten the entire ordeal."

"I don't believe you," Jake chuckled. "You're full of crap, but then again, you usually are."

Both boys busted out laughing. It was a nice moment to help deal with the seriousness of the conversation.

"Seriously," said Jake. "How are you handling this? You can't act like nothing ever happened. I just don't believe you."

"You're right," said Pete. "I'm having problems myself but I may have found a way to deal with them."

"What do you mean?" asked Jake.

Almost nonchalantly, Pete responded. "I want to kidnap those two girls. You know, the Robert's girls. Those pretty girls that live on Route 6, right behind Locust Drive."

Jake sat there, mouth wide open. He really wasn't hearing this. Finally, Jake composed himself and said, "Are you kidding? Cause if you are not kidding, then you are fucking crazy."

"Maybe I am crazy," replied Pete. "I can't sleep or find a job or do much of anything anymore. I want payback. I was never fully convinced Bowman or Casey were guilty and I don't think you were either. Were you?"

"I have always had my doubts," said Jake. "But I have to say, the prosecutor tried to put on a good case. The jury was very emotional. If I was on that jury, I would have convicted them, especially when Casey testified against his buddy."

"Don't you think Casey testified to save his own ass?" asked Pete.

"I suppose so," replied Jake. "Casey was very convincing. He knew most of the details of the kidnapping and shootings."

"Don't you want to know for sure?" asked Pete.

"I don't think so," said Jake. "I still have trouble going outside by myself. I don't think I'm brave enough or strong enough to do something against those two girls. Also, I'm afraid of going to jail. What if we do something and we get caught? Do you want to spend the rest of your life in jail? Do you want to see your name in the News Herald or be a defendant at a trial?"

"No, I don't," responded Pete. "But I can't spend the rest of my life not knowing who took us and murdered our friends."

Pete continued, "I'll tell you what. If you agree to come along with me and we get caught, I will take the entire blame. I'd do it all by myself but I might need a hand controlling the girls."

"That wouldn't be fair to you," said Jake. "I have to think about this. Can you come over tomorrow? Also, I'd like to hear some details of your plan, if you actually have one."

"Yes, I will come over tomorrow and yes, I have a plan," said Pete. "We'll talk more tomorrow. Meet me at the South Kirtland Cemetery tomorrow at noon."

Jake nodded his head in agreement as Pete left the house.

Jake was the first to arrive at the Kirtland Cemetery. While waiting for Pete, Jake was able to reminisce about some of the good times when the boys were younger. Jake thought it was strange to think about good memories while at a cemetery, but he did so nevertheless. Jake remembered playing football in the open stretch of beautiful grass. The grassy area was nearly one hundred yards long and was perfect for football. Many games were played there. Besides football, the boys used the cemetery to play baseball and they also had many BB gun fights.

When Pete finally arrived, he and Jake walked towards the middle of the grassy area and sat down.

"Okay, Pete, what's on your mind?" said Jake.

Pete began, "We need to pull together a plan to kidnap Sally, the youngest girl."

"Seriously, are you off your meds!" exclaimed Jake.

Pete grinned. He remembered all the verbal abuse the boys shelled out to each other. The boys always had lots of fun together.

"No," answered Pete. "I'm as serious as a heart attack."

"So," replied Jake, "What are you going to do once you kidnap Sally?"

"I'm going to force her sister to write a confession," said Pete.

"What are you going to do with the confession?" asked Jake.

Pete responded, "Nothing, not a damn thing. The confession is just for you and I. We both need to know the truth about who kidnapped us and who killed our friends."

"So, you are not going to take the written confession to the police?" asked Jake.

"Nope," replied Pete. "If we bring the confession to the police, they will definitely find out about how we got it. You know, by kidnaping one of the girls. If the police are involved, we could go to prison for a long time."

"Well, I was just wondering about that," said Jake. "I don't want to go to prison. I don't think I can make it in prison."

"Like I told you yesterday, if we are caught, I will take the blame," replied Pete. "I'm willing to go to prison, if only to find out the truth."

"Okay," said Jake. "How do we proceed?"

"I've been thinking and planning this for some time," replied Pete. "There is a little building, no more than a two-car garage, right off Pelton Road in Willoughby. The place is perfect to hold a hostage. I already rented the building."

"Bullshit," said Jake.

"I'm serious," replied Pete. "Do you want to see the building? I have the keys right here."

"I'd love to see the building, but I still think you are full of shit," said Jake.

"Alright, believe what you want," replied Pete. "But we can go right now and talk in the car."

Pete and Jake hopped in the car, a 1964 Impala and drove off towards Willoughby.

Jake was familiar with Pelton Road, a desolate road right off Mentor Avenue.

The boys talked while on the drive about a few of the details regarding kidnapping Sally.

Jake began, "Haven't both the girls met you? For Christ's sake, you took Sally to a dance."

"Yes, I've given this a lot of thought," replied Pete. "I'll tell you why we should take Sally."

"Alright, tell me why," said Jake.

"Couple reasons," replied Pete. "Sally is the youngest and probably the easiest of the two to grab and control. Secondly, Kimberly is the oldest and probably the one to call the shots. If we get a confession, it will most likely come from Kimberly. Finally, Kimberly would probably do just about anything for her little sister. She would not allow any harm to come to her."

"I see your logic," replied Jake. "How do we get into the house?"

Pete replied, "I think we go in through the fruit cellar. During the tour of the farm, Sally showed us the fruit cellar. It's around the backside of the house and it probably gets dark back there"

"You know," said Jake, "Kimberly has a gun. What happens if she pulls a gun on us?"

"She won't be the only person with a gun," said Pete.

Pete pulled a pistol from under his jacket. Jake was beginning to freak out.

"Where the hell did you get that?" asked Jake.

"I borrowed the gun from a friend of mine. That's all you need to know," responded Pete.

Jake asked, "Can you even shoot the gun?

"Ever since Bowman and Casey were released from prison," replied Pete, "I took the gun into the woods and began practicing how to fire it and reload it. I'm actually pretty good with it now. I was never positive who kidnapped us. But, if Bowman or Casey were involved and came looking for me, I wanted to be ready."

Jake shook his head. He wasn't believing everything he was hearing. Jake wondered if maybe he should jump out of the car and run home, but by now the boys were arriving at Pete's rented building.

Jake and Pete went inside to look around. Jake noted there were not any businesses in the immediate area or any homes. The building was totally isolated and probably prefect for the upcoming task.

Pete said, "Over here is the bathroom and toilet. We can chain up one of Sally's feet to a post near the bathroom. That way she can use the toilet when necessary."

Jake sarcastically replied, "Mighty considerate of you."

Pete responded, "Better than having to ring a friggin' bell to go take a leak, isn't it?"

"I guess so," said Jake.

Jake could easily remember the things he and his friends had to endure while being held in dog cages.

"Well, I'm grateful that Sally will be able to walk around and not be confined within a cage," said Jake. "For that I'm really thankful."

Pete replied, "Still, one of us has to stay here with Sally at all times."

"That's stupid," replied Jake. "Why bother to chain her up then?"

"Sally will be wearing a blindfold or a pillowcase at all times," said Pete. "She won't be able to find her way around the building."

"Alright," replied Jake. "What about our voices? Won't she be able to recognize them?" asked Jake.

"I haven't figured that one out yet," said Pete. "Either she has to wear something to cover her ears or we need to disguise our voices. Better yet, we will have some signs already printed up. The signs can say something like, I need to use the bathroom, or I'm hungry. Nothing too specific. We can wear a mask and Sally can take her mask off when she needs something. This way, we never have to speak."

Jake pointed at the garage door of the building. "These windows need to be covered," said Jake. "Maybe we can put some cardboard over them."

"Good idea," said Pete. "That goes on our to-do list." We also need some tape to cover Kimberly and Sally's mouths and some way to knock them out."

"What!" exclaimed Jake. "What do you mean knock them out?"

"I plan on breaking in their house in the middle of the night and taking Sally," said Pete. "We must make sure Kimberly is not a threat. So, we must tie her up, cover her eyes and tape her mouth shut. We don't want to alert their farmhands."

"Well I see you have put a lot of thought into this," said Jake. "Run through the details one more time."

"Alright," replied Pete. "We break into the home around 2:00am when they are sleeping. First, we grab Kimberly and hold her down while covering her eyes then taping her mouth closed so Sally doesn't hear us. Then we go into Sally's room, hold her down, cover her mouth and eyes, then take her to the car. The girls won't know what hit them."

"Then what?" asked Jake.

Pete quickly responded, "I will leave a simple note for Kimberly.

1. Do not call the Police.

2. Do not alert your farmhands.

Then I will leave a note detailing how the confession should look and that we will be in touch with her. Here's what the note should say:

"In the summer of 1963, you kidnapped and tortured four teenage boys. Two of them are dead. You will write a confession of your involvement in this crime. Be sure to include everything you did including why you did it, where the boys were held, what you fed them, how did Tony Sawyer die, how was Kenny Lang murdered, where did you release the remaining boys and what were their names?"

Pete continued, "Also, where did you buy and dispose of the cages and what was your sister's role in this crime? If you contact the police or alert anyone, we will mail your sister home in bite-size pieces. If you refuse to write the confession, you will never see your sister again. If you follow all these details, your sister will be returned unharmed. We will be in contact with you. Stay off the phone."

Jake shook his head in disbelief. He thought nothing good could come from this plan.

Chapter 29

Payback

For the next week, Jake and Pete kept watch on the Robert's farmhouse, writing down all the details they could think of.

The boys discovered Kimberly and Sally went to bed early, around 9:00pm. This was the way the girls were raised and probably still a routine. It made sense. Farm life begins early so the girls would probably be tired early.

Sally was usually the first of the girls to step outside around dawn. Sally would milk the cows and gather the eggs. Even though the work was tedious, Sally was always smiling.

Kimberly came outside an hour after her sister. The boys thought Kimberly was probably cleaning up the breakfast dishes and straightening the house.

The same routine went on day after day. Jake and Pete thought 2:00am would be a perfect time to break into the house.

Finally, the day of the kidnapping came. Jake was sweating up a storm. He was shaking because he was so nervous. Pete took everything in stride. If he was having issues because of their capture and torture, he didn't show it.

Jake said, "Do we have everything? Maybe we should run through this one more time."

Pete sighed, "We've been through this over and over, but we can run through it again if you like."

Jake furiously nodded his head up and down.

"Alright," said Pete. "First, we park the car across the street from their house. Then, we put on our gloves and masks and enter the house from the fruit cellar."

"Okay," said Jake. "I'm with you so far. Then what?"

"Then we sneak upstairs and into Kimberly's room," replied Pete. "Once we are in the room, you hold her down and I will put tape over her mouth and eyes. Then we tie her up and head to Sally's room."

"Maybe you should put the tape over her mouth before I hold her down. That way she can't scream," said Jake.

"That's fine," replied Pete. "Whatever makes you feel more comfortable."

Pete continued, "Once we tie up Kimberly, we go down the hall and get Sally. We do it the same way. We hold her down, tape her mouth, cover her eyes, and then march her out the front door and across the street, into the trunk of the car. We cannot knock out Sally because I don't want to carry her."

Pete glanced down at his watch and said, "It's 2:15. Are you ready?"

"Ready as I will ever be," responded Jake.

The boys exited the vehicle, making their way to the rear of the Roberts' farmhouse.

Pete reached his hand out to open the cellar doors but they were locked. He thought about kicking out a basement window but he did not want to alert the sisters to their intentions.

"Tell you what," said Pete. "Let's go back to the car and wait until they both leave the house. Then we can sneak in without alarming anyone."

"Maybe we can try another door," replied Jake. "I'd like to get this over with while I still have the courage."

The boys walked around the home. Other than the cellar, there were two doors, a side door and a front door. Amazingly enough, the front door was unlocked. Pete turned the door handle and they walked right in. Pete hoped this was not a setup.

Both boys crept up the stairs and soon reached Kimberly's room. Per the plan, Jake pinned Kimberly down by her shoulders as Pete put tape over her mouth. Then Pete put a pillowcase over her head. Kimberly was shaking violently. Pete reared back and punched Kimberly in the side of her head. Kimberly was scared out of her mind and began sobbing. Then Pete taped Kimberly's hands together and secured her to the bed while they went after Sally.

Sally must have heard the commotion because by the time the boys entered her room, she was out of her bed, standing up and alert. Pete didn't plan on this happening. Without hesitation, Pete shined the flashlight right into Sally's eyes, temporarily blinding her, then punched her right upside her head, knocking her unconscious.

Upon entering the room, Sally was already conscious and struggling frantically. She began to fiercely kick at the boys. Not wanting to punch her again, Pete decided it would be best to tie up Sally's feet and carry her. After she was securely bound, Jake threw Sally over his shoulder and headed for the door. Pete stuck his head out of the door to make sure the coast was clear, then brought Sally to the car and threw her in the trunk.

Sally laid in the trunk wondering if Kimberly was injured. She might be in her bedroom, unconscious and bleeding, possibly even dead. Everything happened so fast.

Pete and Jake drove down Route 306, towards Mentor. Neither boy said a word during the entire drive. Once reaching Mentor Avenue, they turned towards

Willoughby and finally turned off on Pelton Road. The entire journey only took twenty minutes. Over the past few weeks, the boys practiced this drive several times. They knew when the Lake County sheriff would be driving through Kirtland and they knew all the posted speed limits along the route.

Pete pulled into the driveway of his garage, then backed up to the door. After parking the vehicle, Pete opened the trunk, slowly at first, then all the way open. Sally was lying very still. Pete hoped she was alright and could breathe. Once again, Jake picked up Sally and carried her into the structure. Pete grabbed Sally's foot, untied it, then clasped it with a metal chain and a padlock. Each boy had one of the keys. Hearing the rattling of the chains shocked Sally and fear set in. Sally began kicking and thrashing around. Jake and Pete put masks over their faces then took the sack off Sally enabling her to see.

Pete held up a sign. It read, *Do as we say and you won't be harmed. If you understand, nod your head up and down.*

Sally nodded her head in agreement.

The next sign read, *If your sister meets our demands, you will be home soon, do you understand?*

Sally nodded her head a second time.

The third sign read, *If we take the tape off your mouth and untie your hands, will you behave?*

Sally immediately began nodding her head up and down.

Pete reached over to Sally and loosened the tape, not quite pulling it off all the way. Then Pete untied Sally's hands, leaving her leg securely chained to a post.

Pete held up the fourth sign. It read, *Do not ask any questions, do not scream or try to yell out, do not cry.*

Sally nodded her head per the previous instructions.

Pete held up the fifth and final sign. It read, *If you need to use the bathroom, just say so. Nobody wants to watch you use the toilet. We will turn around while you do your business. Do you understand?*

Sally nodded her head and said, "Yes, I understand."

Sally had a good idea who may have kidnapped her. She wondered if Pete was involved. She hoped she was wrong, but who else could it be?

Pete left the building to go to work, leaving Jake alone to watch over Sally.

Sally could see the person guarding her was a bigger person. She wondered if this could be Jake Adams, one of the four Kirtland boys she and her sister kidnapped back in 1963. Sally wanted to try to escape before the other person, the mean one, came back.

"I need to use the bathroom," said Sally.

Jake nodded his head and approached Sally then removed the padlock. Jake helped Sally to her feet and showed her to the bathroom. Being a gentleman, Jake turned around so Sally could have some privacy while she used the toilet.

This turned out to be a fatal mistake. Sally stealthily removed the lid from the back of the toilet. Jake still had his back turned on Sally. Earlier, the boys swept the garage for potential weapons but never gave the toilet lid any thought. Jake never saw Sally coming. Holding the toilet lid high over her head, Sally brought the lid down hard on Jake's head, knocking him to the ground. Then Sally continued to hit Jake, repeatedly, until she could hear his skull crack and the sight of blood, lots of blood, flowing all over the bathroom.

Chapter 30

Little Sister

Kimberly was beginning to gain consciousness. Her head was killing her. It felt like she had been hit by a brick on the side of her head. Kimberly began working on the tape on her hands. Little by little she began to free herself. Once she removed the tape binding her hands, she quickly removed the pillowcase and tape across her mouth.

Kimberly rose from the bed and quickly walked into Sally's room. She could see signs of a struggle but Sally was nowhere to be found.

Kimberly walked back to her room and found some cards and notes on her nightstand. She picked up the cards in order and began crying while reading the rules.

Don't call the police. Trust us, don't do it or you will never see your sister alive again.

Don't alert any friends or your farmhands. If you do, you will regret it.

We don't want money.

You will confess to your roles in the kidnapping and torture of four boys and the deaths of Kenny Lang and Tony Sawyer.

The confession must include the following: Why were these boys kidnapped? How were they kidnapped? Where did you take them? How did you hold them? How did Kenny Lang die? How did you dispose of his body? How was Tony Sawyer killed? How did you dispose of his body? Where did you drop the remaining two boys off?

If you refuse to give us this confession, your sister will pay the price.

We will call you. Stay in the house and begin working on your confession.

After reading the instructions, Kimberly began shaking and crying. After composing herself, she went downstairs to make a desperately needed pot of coffee while she paced the floor rapidly, waiting for a call. Suddenly she was overwhelmed with a sensation of pure hatred. She vowed to get her sister back and kill those responsible.

Ring, ring. The sound of the phone ringing sounded as loud as a foghorn in the silent house. Kimberly launched herself at the telephone and answered by the second ring.

"Hello?" said Kimberly, almost whispering.

"We have your sister," said a voice at the other end. "Do you want to see her alive again?"

Kimberly began to respond, "If you lay a hand on my –" The caller cut her off mid-sentence.

"Shut up," replied the caller. "You do not talk unless instructed to do so."

There was dead silence on both ends of the telephone.

The caller continued. "Now do I have your attention?"

Kimberly replied, "Yes, please don't hurt Sally."

"If you follow the instructions, she will be returned safely," replied the caller. "Drink your coffee then start working on your confession."

Kimberly tried desperately to identify the caller, but she could not. There seemed to be something familiar about the voice but she couldn't positively identify it. Maybe it was only the tone that seemed familiar. Maybe it was one of the two remaining Kirtland boys. She knew she should have killed all the boys.

"Can I speak now?" asked Kimberly.

"Speak."

Kimberly felt like a pet waiting for the next command.

"I don't know what confession you're referring to," said Kimberly.

The caller quickly responded, "The next time you deny kidnapping those Kirtland boys, your sister loses a finger. Maybe not a real important finger, but maybe just a little finger or a small toe perhaps. You can decide. Have you called the cops?"

"No sir," replied Kimberly.

"We are watching you," said the caller. "If the police show up at your door, Sally might lose more than just a finger or toe. She will lose an ear or possibly her life. Let me tell you what might happen to your little sister," said the caller. "I will take her to Lake Erie and drive her out, about twenty miles. Once there, I'll chain an anchor around her neck and throw her in the Lake. Unlike Kenny Lang, Sally will still be alive when I toss her in the water."

"Please don't hurt my sister," Kimberly replied while sobbing.

"Then you'd better get to work," said the caller. "Remember, don't leave out any details. I can't wait to read your confession. Time to feed your little sister then maybe have some playtime."

The caller hung up the phone and Kimberly ran to the sink to vomit.

Kimberly had to ask herself some questions. How did the caller know she was making coffee? This alone left Kimberly feeling paranoid. Who was this person? Is it possible it was Pete or the other chubby boy? Maybe it was both boys or maybe one of the parents of either Kenny Lang or Tony Sawyer. Maybe it was Bowman or Casey. They were both just released from prison. Maybe they wanted some payback, but how would they know it was Kimberly and Sally who kidnapped the boys? Kimberly's mind was spinning a thousand miles an hour. She was left with little hope and few options.

Chapter 31

Phone Call

When the phone began to ring, Kimberly nearly jumped out of her skin and hurdled all the furniture just to answer it. "Hello?" said Kimberly.

"Kimmy, it's Sally."

"Oh my God," said Kimberly. "Are you alright? Where are you? Where have you been? Who took you?"

Sally replied, "Simmer down. I'm alright although, I just did something terrible that I can't speak about over the phone. Can you pick me up before I'm caught again?"

"Absolutely," said Kimberly. "Where are you?"

"I'm in Willoughby where Mentor Avenue crosses Pelton Road," Sally replied shakily. "Please come right away!"

"I will be there in 15 minutes," said Kimberly. "Be strong. Also, I'm bringing a gun."

True to her word, Kimberly drove around the intersection of Mentor Ave. and Pelton Road until Sally came out of the shadows, and got into the van.

"Are you hurt?" asked Kimberly.

"I've been better," said Sally. "These animals punched me a couple times until I shut my mouth then they left me alone."

"What is it you couldn't talk about over the phone?" asked Kimberly.

"I talked one of the men into letting me go to the bathroom and when his back was turned around, I hit him over the head with the toilet lid," said Sally. "I beat the crap out of him. I'm sure he is dead."

"Thank god," said Kimberly. "I'm sure he earned it. Do you know who this guy was?"

"Yes," replied Sally. "I know him. It was Jake Adams, the chubby kid we kidnapped before."

"Let's go home and come up with a plan," said Kimberly.

Sally started crying.

"Come on baby," said Kimberly. "You are alright now. I won't let anything else happen to you. I can tell you one thing. Pete is a walking dead man. I will kill him myself. I should have killed all four of them before but I plan to right that wrong."

"Let's just go home," said Sally. "I can't think straight. I need to take a bath and have something to eat. I'm starving."

"How does pizza sound?" asked Kimberly.

"Perfect," answered Sally, as she began to doze off during the drive home.

By the time Kimberly pulled into the driveway, it was starting to get dark outside. The girls went inside the house and Sally took a bath while Kimberly ordered a pizza and drove to pick it up.

Sally came down stairs with her hair wrapped in a towel. The pepperoni pizza was sitting on the table and Sally wasted little time tearing off a slice and quickly consuming it.

By the time Kimberly sat down, Sally was working on her second slice.

Sally glanced up and noticed a shadow hiding behind the curtains.

"Who's there?!" yelled Sally.

Sally's expression alerted Kimberly to a presence. Out from the shadows came Pete Peterson, gun in hand. Pete aimed the gun in Kimberly and Sally's direction.

Staring directly at Sally, Pete said, "I went back to the garage and saw you managed to kill Jake."

Kimberly began to stand up from the table. The first shot rang out, hitting Kimberly directly in the center of her chest. Kimberly fell to the floor. As Pete walked up to her, Kimberly looked at him and said, "Please don't hurt Sally, I'm begging you."

Pete looked at Sally then back down at Kimberly and said, "Why would I hurt Sally? I'm in love with her."

Kimberly looked bewildered and confused. She glanced at her sister, as if to ask why.

Then, Pete lowered the weapon for the final time at Kimberly's head and fired the fatal shot.

Pete pointed the pistol at Sally. He held the gun pointed directly at Sally's face.

"Are you alright?" asked Pete.

"Yes," said Sally. "I'm a little freaked out watching my sister die but you know what, she was a nasty, evil woman and deserved to die. I told her I didn't want to take part in the kidnappings or murders. Nevertheless, after she killed Kenny Lang, she made me help bury him. I didn't want to go to college but again she made me. Kimberly has been telling me what to do my entire life, and I'm sick of it."

"Remind me never to tell you what to do," said Pete. "You are one sick and twisted puppy."

"That's why we make a great couple," replied Sally. "I love you, Pete!"

"I love you too," Pete replied, stroking Sally's hair with the smoking gun still in hand. "Do you know what to do now?"

"Yes," replied Sally. "I will call the police and tell them an intruder shot Kimberly while I hid. Then I will tell them that although I only saw the two men briefly before I hid, they seemed to resemble Bowman and Casey."

"Now that it's dark, I'll head back to the garage and take Jake someplace where I can bury him," said Pete. "It's too bad, all the boys were friends of mine but a man has to look after himself."

Sally smiled and replied, "Starting tomorrow, you are a vested owner in a fruit and vegetable farm. I hear you have some experience!"

Both Sally and Pete laughed out loud.

About the Authors

To date, Donald and Cathy have written six children's books, illustrated in color and available in eBook, Paperback and Audio. This novel, Deadly Pranks, is their first full-length crime mystery book.

Donald and Cathy live in Peoria, Arizona. Cathy is a homemaker and Donald is a retired Manufacturing Manager and former Elementary Governing Board Member in Phoenix, Arizona.

For additional information including ordering and social media links:

Website: www.dcrushbooks.com

Author Page: http://www.amazon.com/-/e/B00B0T04SI

Facebook: www.facebook.com/dcrushbooks

Pinterest: www.pinterest.com/dcrushbooks/

Twitter: www.twitter.com/dcrushbooks

Linkedin: www.linkedin.com/in/dcrushbooks

YouTube: www.youtube.com/c/DCRush

Instagram: www.instagram.com/dcrushbooks/